Carmilla & Laura

Other books by S D Simper:

The Sting of Victory (Fallen Gods 1)
Among Gods and Monsters (Fallen Gods 2)
Blood of the Moon (Fallen Gods 3)
Tear the World Apart (Fallen Gods 4)

Carmilla and Laura

The Fate of Stars (Sea and Stars 1)
Heart of Silver Flame (Sea and Stars 2)
Death's Abyss (Sea and Stars 3)

Forthcoming books:

Eve of Endless Night (Fallen Gods 5) – *2021*
Chaos Rising (Fallen Gods 6) – *2022*
Fallen Gods (Series 2) - TBA
Fallen Gods (Series 3) – TBA

S D Simper

Carmilla and Laura

Copyright © 2018 Endless Night Publications

Cover art by Jerah Moss

ISBN (Paperback) 978-1-7324611-4-7

Visit the author at www.sdsimper.com

Facebook: sdsimper
Twitter: @sdsimper
Instagram: sdsimper

*For my wife, who fell asleep when I
tried reading the original story to her.*

Foreword

I felt entirely unworthy to write this piece.

Anyone who spends more than five minutes with me knows that I love and adore classic literature. I was that weird girl in high school with her head in some obscure fantasy novel, the first to audition for the lead in a Shakespearean play (Which I did land...twice!), and who happily wrote overly prosy essays on the class system in early 19th century France.

Yet, despite being a literary nerd and a lesbian, I'd somehow missed out on Carmilla. I didn't read it until after I'd finished college, and I absorbed it all in one sitting (It's not like it's a long book). I was obsessed. I researched a thousand and one different dissertations written on the gothic horror novella, researched LeFanu himself, the era, the subversion of tropes, the feminist analysis, the impact on history, etc., etc. . . .

Then I started writing words in my head. The impossible thought of expanding on the original narrative buzzed about in my brain for days. One night, I couldn't sleep—I just silently recited passages in my head and splattered them out on my metaphorical canvas the next morning: the scene where our leads first kiss on a moonlit night (Who writes linearly? I wish I did.). From there, I wondered if I had the gumption to move forward, to write this literary love letter to a story I care for so dearly.

As I said, I felt unworthy. But here it is—what I hope is a worthy expansion of themes and story arcs with a little added flavor of my own. As much as I hope to entertain my own audience, I also hope to steer them to the original classic and shed some much-deserved light to the original vampire novella.

Go check out the original tale of Carmilla. But in the meantime, I hope you enjoy this one.

Prologue

"At six years of age, I dreamt of my death."

At midnight, the world sleeps, but airports exist in a pocket of time.

At LAX, Professor Hesselius reads the opening lines of a narrative. She's en-route to France, preparing to speak to the Historical Preservation Board concerning the documents in her lap. She has gone through most of them, but not all, and the ominous opening line pulls a frown to her face.

Found in a mausoleum within the catacombs of a castle in Austria, the journal baffled the gentleman who dug it out—though it bore an old style of French, within the margin was written a line from Sappho, translated from its native Greek:

> *Someone will remember us*
> *I say*
> *Even in another time*

An enlightened bit of poetry to be written in a journal well over a hundred years old.

A sudden bit of cursing draws the professor's attention. A man spills coffee onto his pant leg, and she watches him head toward the nearest restroom. She sees a family of six, the youngest screaming, no doubt exhausted at the late hour. An elderly man with a service dog snoozes two seats away, the dog alert and watching the scene with curious eyes.

The professor returns to her literature, when an announcement is made on the intercom: *AMS to LAX— DELAYED.* A young woman seated in a wheelchair looks up from her copy of *Twilight,* looking crestfallen at the announcement. She sits across from the professor, her dress antiquated but fashionable, hair done up in the lazy sort of bun college-aged girls tend to prefer, and she bears a ring upon her left-hand forefinger.

1

It's a three-hour layover until the plane arrives to take her across the sea. The professor settles in to reread the perilous opener.

At six years of age, I dreamt my death.
I found myself sleepless, the chills of night whispering through my window. I knew no fear. I knew no concept of fear, having been raised on narratives of history and pragmaticism, instead of the fairy tales and ghost stories so often told to children. When the wind sang through my window, I thought only of how my governess sang brighter, her voice a lilt upon the breeze.

In my childishness, I hummed along. I realized, then, I was not alone.

I did not know her, yet I longed to. The woman—hardly a woman; her face was so girlish and young, not a day past eighteen—held a visage as luminous as the moon beyond and eyes as dark as the sky itself. She stood by the windowsill, face full of wonder as she looked upon my childish form, dressed in lace and silk. When she caught my eye, her humming ceased. Instead, she stepped forward, arms outstretched.

Not one of her steps made a creak upon the floor. The woman stopped before my bed, and I swore I saw immutable sorrow on her face, her eyes glistening in the dim light. "The time has not yet come," she whispered, her voice as soft as the moonbeams upon the windowsill.

I knew not of what she spoke, and instead I curled into my sheets. The woman dropped her hands. I sensed her sorrow, felt it down in the depths of my young heart, and longed to wipe her threatened tears. I loved her, though I did not know her.

I beckoned her forward.

In gentle, trepid measures, she crawled in bed beside me. The warmth of her embrace as she engulfed my youthful form stayed with me in dreams for years to come. Wetness stained my blonde locks; her grip tightened as she drew comfort from my presence. She whispered, muffled by the thick waves of my hair, "Darling, darling—how I've missed you."

God spoke of angels coming to watch us in the night. I wondered, in my innocence, if this strange and beautiful specter were one such as they, my own mother, perhaps, she having passed on to heaven when I had scarcely learned to walk. My arms wrapped around her, my face buried in the collar of her dress, and I breathed in the scent of earth upon her skin.

Lips brushed the top of my head. I looked up—

I shrieked at the nightmare. From her eyes streaked tears of blood, staining her face in ghastly shades of black and red. Fangs peaked from her parted lips. Her embrace, once a comfort, became a cage. I beat against her with my tiny fists, imploring her to *release me*—

I awoke screaming. Sunlight bathed my room in warmth, birds singing to dampen my cries, but still I screamed until the door burst open. Madam Perrodon rushed in, the ties of her nightgown loose and flowing behind her. "Laura—!" I sobbed into my hands. "Laura!" she cried, and she fell at my bedside, trembling as she attempted to uncover my face. "My child, what has happened?!"

I dared not speak my vision. Great droplets of tears fell from my eyes as she frantically searched my skin for wounds.

And so entered Mademoiselle De Lafontaine, the second of my governesses, and thereafter, my father, roused by my shrieks and those of Perrodon. As the two women attended to me—women I had known since my infancy—my father searched the window and the bed, perhaps seeking signs of intruders.

"There are no marks upon her," proclaimed De Lafontaine, relief in her voice. "Monsieur, she is not hurt."

I recalled the specter's tears, knew they must have stained my bed and hair, but saw nothing, felt nothing. My father sat before me and pulled me into his arms, giving no care that my tears stained the expensive fabrics of his morning coat. "Laura," he said, and even as a child, I heard his fear, "you are safe now." He kissed my cheek and held me, protective and tight. "Tell us what you remember."

And so I told him—of my sleeplessness, of the woman in the night, and of her fangs, her face, stained with blood. I blubbered and sobbed all the while, for I remembered her sorrow and felt it as my own.

"Laura," he chided, though with kindness on his tongue, "it was a dream. Only a dream." Then, he turned to Madam Perrodon. "Call the doctor."

The doctor arrived in the early afternoon. My composure had returned, spurred by my father's presence and a full stomach. An older man, his white hair hardly a wisp upon his head and with evidence of small pox scars upon his lined face, introduced himself. "I am told you had a scare last night," he said, kneeling by my bedside. "Laura, will you open your mouth wide for me?"

He inspected my mouth, my throat, my ears, and when there was no evidence of discord, he inspected my skin for superficial wounds, especially my neck. As he did, he asked me to relay my dream, and I told him all, though with fewer hysterics.

"She is healthy," the doctor told my father, "but may we speak in the hallway a moment?"

Perrodon sat at my bedside as they spoke in the hallway, but she and I both strained to listen when my father suddenly shouted, "Are you mad?"

Whatever the doctor said was drowned beneath my father's cry of, "Then Baron Vordenburg is mad as well! What you speak of is supernatural!"

He returned shortly and said, "Doctor Spielsburg insists we call the priest."

When the priest arrived, he smiled and said, "Laura, how you've grown!"

I was baptized in my infancy by Father Dubois, or so said my father—I did not recall the man. "Thank you for coming," my father told him, and once they had greeted the other, Father Dubois came to my bedside.

If I could turn the tables of time, I would have said nothing, or at least shied from the details of what I told myself was all a dream. But children are honest, and I told him all—of the woman and the words she spoke, of her embrace, and of her fangs.

His frown only deepened as the story progressed. Finally, I stopped, apprehensive at his displeasure. "Am I in trouble?"

Immediately, his countenance changed to something merry, forced as it might have been. "No, Laura, no. Dreams are merely that—dreams. Figments of our imagination. Our Lord will not hold us accountable for such."

I knew it was no dream. When I shut my eyes, I still felt the warm of her embrace, smelled the earthen scent of her skin. But the priest reached out and gently touched my neck as the doctor had done, a curious frown across his face as he inspected my skin. "Madam, will you pull down the child's collar?"

Perrodon did so, and the doctor kept his scowl as he inspected my collar and chest. "Do you recall any pain? Any sting?"

I shook my head.

He stood and went to my window. From his bag, he produced a metal flask, one that reflected the sun's light. A few droplets fell to his fingers, and he anointed the water upon the windowsill, sprinkled it upon the ground, and then to the wooden posts of my bed.

"Will you pray with me, Laura?"

I gestured the sign of the cross in tandem with he and my father, who knelt beside Father Dubois. I shut my eyes and heard him speak—words of comfort, words of protection, a blessing for the fearful of heart.

He bid me farewell.

Madam Perrodon insisted upon sleeping on the rocking chair at my bedside that night—*"For your comfort, Laura. We would not want you to awaken alone and frightened."*—and so passed an uneventful sleep. No dreams of supernatural visitors; no women in my bed.

I feared her, yet I never forgot her face. It had burned itself into my mind, and though I stopped entertaining the memory in time, even convinced myself it merely *had* been a figment of my imagination, in the darkest parts of the night I saw her behind my eyelids—her sorrow and her beauty both.

Chapter One

In my nineteenth year, I awoke to a fluttering of excitement in my heart.

The sun had scarcely risen, casting tranquil beams of light across my bed. Birds sang a chorus to chime in the morning, and I sat up, unable to help my radiant smile. For a blissful moment, I simply breathed, content to bask in the calm before the perfect storm, overjoyed to know that my resigned loneliness would come to an end.

A knock at the door disturbed my peace, but it brought no ire. "Come in," I said, unsurprised when Madam Perrodon entered. Her face was one I had known all my life, though gray had come to streak the bun of her hair. She kept a prim manner of dress, and though the buttons of her bodice stretched at the seams for her weight, her cheery disposition covered all number of flaws.

"I thought you might need some help taming that hair of yours," Perrodon said, smiling as she sat on the bed beside me. Before I could comment, her expert fingers began untying the many strips of fabric bunched into my hair. It matched the color of the sun, reflecting its light when it fell from her hands. Curls were the style of the times, or so I'd been told—I hadn't travelled far enough to know.

"Thank you," I said, making no move to assist her— past experience said I would only irrevocably tangle the blonde curls. "I know it's a silly thing, but I want to impress her."

Perrodon's laugh matched the cadence of the birds outside. "My dear, Mademoiselle Rheinfeldt will adore you no matter how you style your hair."

"I do hope so," I replied, transfixed at the foreign feeling of the curled locks. I shook my head, grinning at how they bounced against my cheeks.

Perrodon continued her work, but with each second, anticipation only grew, as though her hurry would make the time pass sooner. Once my hair was freed, she styled it back from my face and tied it loosely with a bow.

I dressed clumsily, fingers trembling from excitement as my governess helped to cinch me into my bodice. "How tight do they keep their corsets in Vienna?"

Oh course, she knew my thoughts. "The mademoiselle will not care how tightly you cinch your corset." For all her prim proclivities, Perrodon was practical above all else. "No need to suffocate yourself when there are no gentlemen to impress."

"The general would surely accompany his ward."

I had no reason to impress General Spielsdorf, given that he was near my father's age, but Madam Perrodon acquiesced nonetheless.

With each tug on the strings, I swallowed a whine and prayed Perrodon paid no mind to my grimace. It became an internal battle of wills—my desperation for acceptance steadily losing to the panic of shattering my ribs. In the mirror, my waist shrunk by pained degrees, until Perrodon blessedly said, "You'll scare the mademoiselle if you greet her like this—you look like a ghost, with as white as you've turned."

When she loosened it, I was relieved to see I resembled a human girl once more, instead of a vase. "Hopefully tight enough for Vienna," she said with a wink, then she helped me to don my pastel dress.

I said nothing, instead keeping my joy contained. Underneath layers of skirts, I ran from her, no farewell but her laughter.

My father owned a rich estate, having been born to fortune and inheriting all my maternal grandfather had, including a castle at the outskirts of the forest Styria, my mother's homeland. Entire rooms had been shut away, furniture covered in sheets to protect them from dust, for it was only he and I, my governesses, and a small collection of servants.

My footsteps echoed across the polished stone, passing carpeted rooms and furniture more ancient than the home itself. My late grandfather had been a connoisseur of art, but I hardly noticed the collections anymore—the statues, the paintings, all of them lining the walls and creating rich centerpieces. My heeled shoes and stockings echoed as I sped down the stairs, past the entry hall and chandelier, when I finally saw my father in the drawing room.

He immediately snuffed his cigar, though the smoke lingered, swirling in the designs of nouveau before dissipating into the ceiling. My father smelled of smoke and tobacco, familiar and warm. Before he looked up from his paper, he released a violent cough into his handkerchief. "Pardon me," he said, finally smiling at my entrance. "Good morning, Laura. You look ready to present yourself before the ball."

He jested, but I grinned. "Any news?"

"You'll be the first to know."

My morning prayers, instead of quiet, self-centered pleas for excitement, were of gratitude. I busied myself, anticipation brewing with every passing hour. My twitching earned the ire of Mademoiselle De Lafontaine. "Laura, pay attention," she said as we sat at my writing desk. "Proper German syntax won't be found staring out the window."

"Yes, mademoiselle." Still, I listened for the distant crunching of rocks beneath heavy carriage wheels.

Mademoiselle De Lafontaine was all lines and angles, accentuated by her plaid dress—the height of Parisian fashion, or so she said. But she exclusively wore funeral tones, the only bit of finery the cross around her neck. "And tighten your corset. If you can slouch, it is too loose."

Madam Perrodon chuckled at her chide. "Let her be. She hardly needs it anyway."

I read, I wrote, I ate, I paced . . .

Sunset fell, and my father called for me.

He stood before his desk, frowning at some piece of opened mail. "Laura, come outside a moment."

No joy in his countenance; only a forced stoicism I could not fathom the source of. I nodded and watched him slip the letter into his back pocket as he followed me back to the entry hall and to the outside.

The manor sat upon a lush, grassy field, surrounded by groves of trees and stone paths navigating the expansive grounds. Flowers dotted the bushes before us, lined the stone path from the road to the house itself, but my father stepped off and into the grass.

He offered his arm. I accepted, anxiety growing at what I knew could only be terrible news.

Through the field of grass, we approached the maintained dirt road and walked along the side of it in silence. Beyond the road and the trees before us, I could make out the beginnings of an expansive lake, yet another facet of my father's inheritance. It sparkled in the setting sun, nearly blinding, but the final vestiges of sunlight vanished. The moon would rise; at the midnight hour, mist would settle and cover the lake.

Such was the Forest of Styria—by day a paradisiacal glory, as Virgil himself would say; by night it fell to darkness all-consuming, the moon casting rays of ghostly lights that scarcely broke through the trees.

I'd never dared to come alone. But with my father, and the sword at his hilt, I felt no fear. Fog descended like a suffocating cloud as we walked toward the lake. My father finally said, "I received a letter from General Spielsdorf this afternoon. He has been detained, perhaps another two months."

Like a knife had sunk into my back, my excitement steadily drained away. "Did he say why?"

My father's hesitation spoke volumes; he was not a man to mince words. "He must make new arrangements in light of a tragedy. His ward, Bertha Rheinfeldt, passed away."

The knife dug deeper, this time piercing my heart. "But—" My steps ceased, suddenly lacking the strength to move. I stared up into my father's forlorn countenance. "How? Not six weeks ago, he wrote that she had been struck by a fainting spell, but—"

I had to stop. Tears welled in my eyes as my father's arms wrapped around me. To cry would do nothing, not for Bertha, stolen from this world too soon. But selfishly, my tears fell in rapid droves. Loneliness, and the resignation of it, swamped my broken heart. She would have stayed only a month or two, but it would have been time spent with company—with a friend to cherish. Now, I felt I had lost something I'd never even held.

For not the first time, I wondered what it would mean to leave this place. The comforts of home brought contentment, yes, but I longed for companionship.

Father's home held empty rooms, as lonely as my own self.

"My tender-hearted Laura," he said, rubbing his hand along my back. "Perhaps a trip to town is due. Tomorrow, you and I can go and take our minds off this tragedy."

I offered a nod, though I knew it was a poor recompense.

Through my father's muffling jacket, I heard the crunching of gravel beyond, and had my heart not been shattered moments ago I would have assumed it to be our guests. Few came this way, especially at this hour. I pulled away and, curious, I approached, my father behind me. Surely he felt the same.

Coming from the nearby hill, I saw a large carriage. Four horses pulled it along, their speed ever-increasing, and even in the fading light I saw the oddness of its driver. The palest man I had ever seen, wearing the garb of a gentleman yet deathly thin, skeletal in his features—

Horses screamed. Wood creaked and shattered. The carriage veered off the road toward the lake and toppled over. Forgetting my own tragedy, I ran to the cacophony, though my father arrived much sooner, unhindered by voluminous mountains of skirts and a great metal cage around his ribs.

The carriage lay on its side, and as my father reached it, the coachman seated at the back and the driver—each as ghastly as the other—ran toward the door. It faced the sky, entirely on its side, and with my father's help they pulled open the heavy carriage door.

A hand took my father's. From the overturned carriage emerged a woman nearing middle-aged, but beautiful, utterly flawless aside from the laughter lines at her eyes and cheeks. Pins held her fine, black hair in a sort of swirl, like the seashells decorating our mantlepiece, and her skin matched the moon's hue. She nearly fell into my father's arms, trying to retain her balance. "Monsieur, thank you," she said, in perfect French, but she kept her stare on the carriage door.

The two servants emerged from the toppled carriage, carrying what appeared to be an unconscious young woman. I watched for scarcely a moment before they laid her to rest beside the carriage, at the shore of the lake.

"'Tis a miracle you did not fall into the water," my father replied.

Behind them, the coachman and the driver moved about to calm the horses, helping them rise with a strength their gaunt forms should not have possessed. But my father seemed to not notice, his attention kept to the woman instead. "This is a stroke of ill fate," she said, staring with pursed lips between the carriage and the road. "Forgive me my frustration, Monsieur, but I have been summoned and must make haste, yet I fear my daughter will not have the strength to travel. She is a fragile girl; sound of mind but weak of heart. She will need to rest after such a scare."

At her words, a strange and sudden hope filled me. An idea, perhaps ill-conceived and certainly impulsive, struck me. I tugged on my father's sleeve, and when he turned I whispered, "Father, if the girl is too sick to travel, let her stay with us."

"Madam," my father said, no lapse in his words, "if it pleases you, it would be no trouble for your daughter to stay in my home and be a companion to mine."

"Monsieur, I cannot ask so great a favor of you. I do not know you." She looked with some forlorn at the still figure lying on the bank. "You must understand, it will be three months before I am able to return."

My father shook his head, and my heart felt a bit of fluttering joy. "No trouble, Madam. Not this morning, we received news that the ward we had agreed to house will no longer be coming. Perhaps this is fate."

"Fate, indeed," the woman replied. "Excuse me a moment, then."

I watched her step away and kneel before the girl by the lake's edge.

My father's hand appeared at my back. "Perhaps this is a recompense to you, my Laura." He smiled, and I thought he may be right. My heart ached for Bertha's passing, but my own selfish prayers were fulfilled.

The woman returned, her countenance much lighter. "My daughter has agreed to stay with you. I have given her instructions, and I will give the same request of you—do not ask her of my quest, nor of her history. She is easily startled. But I give you my word, Monsieur, that all will be explained upon my return in three months."

My father gave a quick nod, though I felt the stiffening of his hand on my back. An odd request, indeed. "Your daughter will be cared for as my own. And by my own." He smiled at me reassuringly, then gave a slight push on my back.

I stepped forward, heart palpitating at the prospect of this new guest. I could not ask who she was or where she was from, but still I wondered—was she from a great city? Was she fashionable? Oh, would she think me some naïve country girl—?

All self-conscious thoughts vanished when I saw her face. With fluttering eyelashes, she looked up and met my gaze, her enormous, dark eyes immediately growing bright. Hers was a beautiful face—ethereal, even—soft and pristine, not a blemish on her features. She smiled, her lips full and red, juxtaposing vibrantly with her skin, white as milk, and offered a hand. I took it, too enthralled to speak, and found it dainty and frail.

Here was the woman—the one who missed me and proclaimed the time had not yet come, who held me in her arms and wept. I knew her face. Those lips had touched my hair.

But the figment of my dream had held immutable sorrow. This woman—this girl, for she was no older than myself—smiled with a radiance to dull the sun.

I helped her rise. The black lace of her dress spoke of finery with its high collar and long, puffed sleeves— fashionable, yes, but perhaps impractical for summertime.

I could not shake the image of her countenance from the one in my nightmare and it irked me so.

Needless to say, I gasped when she suddenly threw her arms around me, giggling with girlish delight. "Tell me your name, please," she said, and I stiffened when she placed a kiss upon my cheek. Her lips did not leave; instead, she leaned toward my ear and whispered. "A secret for a secret."

"Laura," I replied, and I swore the blush at my cheek burned brighter than the moonlight reflected from the lake.

She pulled back, her slight hand caressing my cheek. "You may call me Carmilla—"

"Carmilla!"

The woman's sharp cry broke the enchantment between us. "Remember yourself," the woman continued, and her expression remained stern. "I must take my leave."

Carmilla smiled, though with hardly the same enthusiasm she had gifted me. "Farewell, Momma," she said, and waved.

The carriage had righted. I saw Carmilla's mother and my father exchange quick words, but I heard nothing—Carmilla looked back to me, stole my hands, and said, "This is a wonderful twist of fate."

She was so dramatic in her words and expressions, her eyes alight with joy. "I think I agree," I said, for what else could I say, even if she wore the face I feared? And truly, it would be a delightful few months—it was all I had wanted, a companion my age. Yet, even aside from her eerie familiarity, something in her touch and smile pulled revulsion from my stomach.

But I could not look away. Nor did I think I wanted to, even if impulse whispered to run.

I heard wheels on dirt and saw the carriage pull away. No further farewells—Carmilla's mother left without another word, and all that was left was my father and a large suitcase.

She seemed a cold woman.

Carmilla kept my hand as she pulled me toward her suitcase—which my father carried. "I tire quickly," she said, and already I saw how she swayed. Perhaps this explained her odd affection—desperation for support, more than the impulse for friendship.

So, I obliged—I placed my hand at her waist, using my strength to help her walk along the path back to the manor.

Every new thing excited her—she gasped upon seeing my father's home and proclaimed it too beautiful for words, waving her hands about to express her enthusiasm. I told her there was much to explore around the grounds, and she insisted she see it all, once she had recovered.

Still, Carmilla looked near collapsing when we stepped inside. My father must have noticed too. "Are you hungry, Carmilla?"

"Merely exhausted," she said, wistful as she visibly reveled in the décor. "But I don't believe I can sleep—not yet. Perhaps some tea to calm my nerves?"

My father ran ahead to inform the cook of our new guest. Alone, I escorted her, my hand still at her waist, and felt her weight slowly grow heavier. She matched me in height, yet there was a frailty to her we did not share. Her build held the sort of softness that came from sickness, from spending precious time in bed instead of out in the world.

Camilla remained enthralled by every new thing. "What beautiful décor! Oh, such wonder!" Her smile grew wide at the chandelier, her delight palpable upon seeing the statues and paintings. "There must be stories for each of them."

"A few, I think," I replied, wary of her enthusiasm. "You would have to ask my father."

"And I shall!" she proclaimed, and she threw her hands into the air and laughed. "Forgive me, Laura, but I'm overjoyed to be staying here. Your home is a mystery I long to explore."

I smiled and escorted her to the parlor.

We learned little of our impromptu guest, giving regard to the strange vow she had made. But she learned all about us and listened with rapt attention, asking questions and charming us both with her laugh and smile.

Yet, I could not disregard the simmering discontent in my stomach, the memory of her face pulling thoughts of a warm embrace and a blood-stained face. I could not fathom what this meant, what trickery my mind had pulled—or was it she herself?

But to accuse her of being some witch or demon would be a cruel thing, especially with nothing but a childish dream for proof.

Upon finishing her tea, she expressed her desire to sleep. My father asked me to escort her.

I stole a candle and helped her to stand, and again she gazed at me with adoration. I wondered if her frailty simply led to starry-eyed gratitude toward whomever she met. "We have a room set up," I said, keeping my hand at her waist. She leaned into the touch, letting me take most of her weight. Her dark, brunette hair fell across my shoulder in curled waves, threatening to tangle with mine. "Will you be all right alone? I can stay at your bedside and read."

Carmilla shook her head. "I must tell you, I am deathly terrified of intruders." When we reached the stairs, I helped her to step up, one by one. "Once, as a child, my home was broken into by thieves, and now I cannot bear the feeling of sleeping when I feel someone's presence. Although . . ." Halfway up the stairs, she stopped, and I feared a moment she would fall. Instead, her hand braced the banister, the candlelight casting gaunt lines across her pristine face. "It may not be so awful, if it is only you who sits beside my bed."

"I will allow no one else," I replied, the oddity of her request still settling into my mind. I took her hand when she had steadied and helped to pull her the rest of the way.

On the second floor, all the curtains were drawn. The candle flickered, the eerie shadows of décor and ancient stone busts greeting us. Fortunately, Carmilla seemed to have passed her dizzy spell, walking easily on her own, though with languid slowness. "What happened to your other guest?"

"I beg your pardon?"

"There was another girl meant to stay here," Carmilla explained, visibly enthralled by the paintings upon the wall. Her large eyes gazed upon each one, despite the dim light.

Though the sadness had muted, the loss still prickled somewhere in my mind. "We received news this morning that she had passed away, actually."

"Oh, heavens!" Carmilla exclaimed, and she stopped in her tracks and wrapped her arms around me. I *swore* I'd felt that soft embrace before, curled around me in my bed. "I am terribly sorry to hear it."

She caressed my waist as she released me, the gesture familiar from others, yet drawing a foreign sort of intimacy from her, a shock that ran through my blood. Carmilla held only my hand now, and I felt it were her leading me along.

We reached the room set aside for Mademoiselle Rheinfeldt, but now for Carmilla, and when I opened the door, she squealed with delight. With radiant excitement, she clapped her hands as she stepped inside, giggling.

From anyone else, her dramatics might have been ridiculous. Yet from her, it fit the ever-growing puzzle of this eccentric young woman. "Such a beautiful room! You and your father are too kind to me."

She left my side, and with careful steps she approached the suitcase on the floor beside her bed. I watched her kneel before it, her small hands carefully unlatching the straps. "Will you open the curtains? I do so love the moonlight."

I obeyed wordlessly, pulling the expansive, maroon curtains apart. With the candle secure upon the windowsill, I tied the curtains with gold ribbons, the room now lit by moon and fire.

"Would you help me? Please?"

I looked up and saw Carmilla struggling with the buttons at the back of her black dress. In trepid motions, I approached, brushing against her fingers as I steadily detached each button down the line, revealing the steel-boned corset and underclothes.

When I helped her step from the dress, I hesitated to go further, unsure of the uncomfortable pit in my stomach. Instead, I carefully set the dress upon the bed, folding it with the same care I had seen my father's servants perform in the past.

"Are you always so quiet?" I heard her ask, the edge of laughter on her voice.

I had heard nothing but radiance from her all day, and with my own discontentment, I realized it irked me. Releasing a sigh, I turned toward her, shy at the revealed cleavage of her underclothes. Had it been so long since I'd seen another woman that I would shy even at something so terribly non-scandalous?

Yet, she was so unendingly beautiful. Perhaps I felt inadequate—jealously gave rise to prickling discomfort, yes? "I apologize," I said, and proceeded to struggle with the knots at her waist. In nineteen years, I'd never been expected to remove a corset; instead the honor had fallen to Madam Perrodon. Yes, I'd felt it done a thousand times, but when the cords finally fell at her waist, I hesitated before tugging at the strings for fear of jostling the frail girl.

And of appearing a fool.

Apparently she mistook my hesitation. "If this is below you, it will not offend me if you call someone to help. I grew up with a great many servants—I do understand."

"I'm not bothered," I said, then swallowed my pride and added, "only confused."

Her musical laughter brought light into the dim room. "I see. Pull the strings—start from the middle and move out. But be gentle, please. It doesn't do well to jostle a lady as you undress her."

By God, her tone irked me, but I obeyed. It had not been cinched tight, and for that, I was grateful—every moment with her hastened my blood. My fingers trembled as they loosened the strings along her back, until suddenly her own hands unclasped the pieces up front. The corset fell into my hands.

Once removed, she bent over to remove her bustle and layers of skirts.

She did not deserve my ire, this lovely girl in my home. And so, I chose to confess. "Carmilla, I would be plain with you. And what I will say will sound insane." When she stepped from her petticoats, I gathered them myself. She wore nothing but a white chemise, the fabric thin enough for me to see the palest hints of her skin beneath—though her own pigmentation was hardly a shade darker. Her large eyes held mine as she tucked herself into bed. "But I've seen your face before."

"Have you?" she asked, and she hardly breathed the words.

"I would swear before the priest that I saw you . . ." Hesitation rose in my throat, but I fought the innate fear of her judgement and spat the words. ". . . in a dream."

Recognition flashed through her eyes. Her full lips pulled wide into a smile. "I feared your judgement to say it, but my darling, I swear I could say the same. I saw you—by God, thirteen years ago!"

I sat at her bedside and did not shy when she took my hand. "It was," I said, breathless at her words. "It was thirteen years ago. I was six." I told her of my vision, of she herself at my window, sorrowful and lonesome, and how she stole me into her arms and cried in my embrace.

Carmilla listened with rapt attention. I spared mention of her fangs—for fear of causing offense—but emphasized the realness of it, the vibrant detail. "In time, I convinced myself, that it was my imagination, but if I shut my eyes, I remember it as clear as the windowpane. I know it is insane—"

"Not insane," Carmilla said, and she squeezed my hand, the gentleness in her gaze threatening to break down some invisible wall I had never known existed. "My dearest Laura, my vision was the same, yet *I* was the woman who held you that night. I recall it clear as day, that I awoke in your bedroom, that I saw you lying in your bed and my heart, my heart—" I heard her breath hitch, as though overwhelmed. "It *ached*. I did not know you, yet I missed you like you were a part of my own soul torn away. And when you beckoned for me—" She held my hand tight, and I swore her eyes glistened, just as the woman in the dream. "I had never felt such joy."

I cringed, but I had to ask, "Forgive me, but do you recall any blood?"

"Yes, I do—the horror of it all." Carmilla's hand waved the words away. Her fingers stroked my hand, as though drawing her own comfort from my skin. "I recognized you the moment you appeared before me by the lakeside. I felt I had missed you all my life. Surely this is fate—you and I were meant to be."

I smiled at the thought, oddly relieved to know she had been plagued by a similar, nightmarish vision. I wondered at the sorcery, if this were God or something wicked, but a truth in her words resonated against my heart: fate decreed she come here to find me.

She brought my hand to her face, kissing it in the manner of a gentleman, and I wondered at her forward, passionate gestures. Hers were the actions of a woman in a haze of ardor, so precise and yet enthused, senseless even.

I wondered at her thoughts, if there were some male suitor awaiting her return. When she brought my hand down, I stole it away. "Do you still wish for me to stay at your bedside?" I asked, oddly relaxed in her presence now, entranced by the softness of her as she settled between the sheets.

"You're kind to offer," she said, her smile as serene as the clouds passing over the moon. "But you ought to sleep as well. I should warn you; I am prone to sleep until well into the day. Do not feel like you must wait for me— you may not see me until the afternoon," she finished with a laugh.

"Should I awaken you for meals?"

"I need sleep much more than I need food," Carmilla said, and already I saw weight pulling at her eyelids, her long lashes fluttering. "Though I would ask, when you leave, that you lock the door behind you. My fear of intruders is quite irrational, especially in a home such as this, but if you would not mind—"

"It would be no trouble," I interrupted, my heart softening at her rambled apology. What a life she must live, to be in ill health. Yet she seemed so admirably full of vibrancy, nonetheless.

I stood and stole the candle from the windowsill and listened as her breaths grew steady and deep. They were hardly audible at all, but when I glanced over at her bed, she seemed at peace, the radiant smile on her lips softer, more relaxed.

How beautiful she looked in the flickering candlelight—her white skin took on the same faint glow, casting an almost rosy hue upon her cheeks. It sparkled against her dark hair, highlighting the golden strands within, coloring them a glistening auburn.

Such peace in her visage. "Goodnight, Carmilla," I whispered at the door.

As I gently shut the door, I heard a treasured tone say, "Goodnight, my Laura."

Father's house had always been quiet. Not peaceful, no—but quiet.

I swore I lived among a sea of ghosts, of forgotten memories and stagnant stillness. My father spoke glowingly of the days when my mother had walked the halls—so vibrant was her joy, he said. She filled the halls with light and life and brought warmth wherever she went. Her presence had filled the entire home and made it feel less . . . cold.

But she had gone, and I was a paltry replacement, much too shy to fill our home with my presence. Instead, days would pass without spotting any one of my father's servants. They, too, were among the spectral figures in my life—silent and aloof. Not forbidden from speaking to me, no, but I was demure, and they had their duties. After nineteen years of silence, my life hardly felt like a living, breathing world, but a bubble of time, the passage shown only in the graying strands of my father's hair and my own growth from child to young woman.

In the morning, I saw no sign of our guest. Carmilla had not exaggerated—after breakfast and morning prayers, I resisted the urge to awaken her, recalling her fear of intruders.

I set myself up in the upstairs study, content to practice writing in German and thus please Mademoiselle De Lafontaine. Still, she did not emerge.

By lunch, I was skittish, and finally, though it was not expected of me, sat at my desk to practice my English instead.

I know not how many hours passed, only that Madam Perrodon finally came to check on me, with dinner and a small glass of wine. "I expected you to be with Mademoiselle Carmilla," she said, placing the meal beside me on the heavy oak desk.

"She has been asleep all day," I replied, setting aside my writing. Study led to ravenous hunger. "Her health is poor, and after the scare last night, she needed time to recover."

"A pity. I hoped to meet her; your father says she is quite charming."

I nodded, for it was true.

Our conversation turned to tutoring my English— *"You'll be a poet in no time, dear! Now, if only your German was as well rehearsed."*—and when the sun had nearly set, I heard the door creak open.

Perrodon and I both turned in tandem, and I smiled upon seeing Carmilla watching from the doorway. She wore the same chemise, but covered with a deep green robe, and her stance suggested she had gained some strength. "Good evening," she said, glancing between the two of us. Her skin reflected the candlelight, pure and white and now flickering with fire.

Madam Perrodon immediately stood and approached. "So you are Carmilla!" She swept Carmilla into a hug, the matronly woman engulfing the soft, waifish girl. "It is a joy to have you here. I am Madam Perrodon, Laura's governess."

Visibly startled, as Perrodon released her, Carmilla said, "I'm quite charmed to be under your roof."

"Are you feeling better? Laura says you had a scare last night."

Carmilla nodded, glancing to me at every other word. "Sleep has helped the worst of it. I plan to lie down again soon, but I thought to come say hello first."

She stepped past Perrodon, her hair flowing free behind her and tucked by her shoulders. It held the remnants of its earlier curls, but smoother now, shined and soft. It brushed past my face as she leaned over beside me. Her other hand slid up my shoulder, where it lingered, her thumb drawing circles against the fabric. "What are you working on?" Before I could answer, she glanced down and grinned, then began to recite the English words upon the page with perfect pronunciation: *"The full-orbed moon with unchanged ray mounts up the eastern sky . . ."*

"I did not know you spoke English," I said, charmed at her words.

"And I did not know you liked poetry," she replied, her eyes still roaming the page.

"Writing out the text helps me to understand them better. I've come to love American poets," I admitted, and I could not help my blush when she laughed.

"I find that adorable. You are *adorable*, my darling," she said, palpably enthused. Her lips brushed my cheek, her chaste kiss darkening my blush. She pulled away, and I found that I missed her.

From the door, Perrodon chuckled and said, "It seems you two are quite taken with each other. It has been much too long since there has been another girl to keep Laura company."

"She and I will be dear to each other," Carmilla said, and she sat beside me, in the Madam's chair. "I look forward to every day and night to come."

"I will leave you two alone, then," Perrodon said. "It is wonderful to meet you, Mademoiselle Carmilla."

She left us, and suddenly the weight of Carmilla's presence, of she and I alone together, began to settle. As though she read my thoughts, Carmilla's head came to rest upon my shoulder. "Forgive me; I did not intend to rest all day," she whispered. "I'll surely sleep all night. But I hope it does not startle you to say I missed you."

It did, but not for annoyance. Instead, I was intimately aware of her hair tickling my neck, of her arm as it wrapped around mine, our skin brushing together. I said nothing, unable to unravel the meaning of this rope she tied around me, for I was enthralled by her presence.

"Will you keep writing? I do not mind if you work."

I reached for my pen, but as my finger went to grab it, her thumb brushed my arm, and even through the fabric I swore it struck me like lightning. Clumsily, it fell, and in my panic I said, "I apologize. I-I am much too nervous to work while you watch."

"I would never judge you—"

"A-Actually, I think I am quite tired," I said instead, and when I pulled away, she released me.

I saw hurt in her large eyes, some hope extinguished. I dared not consider it more; there was no mystery.

So, why should she be wounded? I had done nothing. Yet, her pitiful stance lacerated some tender thing inside me. Desperate to salvage her happiness, I asked, "Are you hungry?"

The hint of a smile reappeared on her red lips. "No. Mademoiselle De Lafontaine was kind enough to introduce herself and escort me to the kitchen. She directed me here."

"Do you need escorted to your room, then?"

"I would appreciate that."

I helped her to stand, and she kept hold of my hand as I led her away, stealing the candle from the study to light our path. It illuminated the hallway in eerie shadows, and I shied away at the mirrors and the pictures on the walls, unwilling to admit my fear of ghosts and subtle horrors. Our footsteps echoed across the stone floors and walls, and when we finally reached Carmilla's room, I said, "You may take the candle with you, if you like."

She shook her head. "I see well enough in the dark."

I had accomplished one useful task that day. From my pocket, I withdrew a key. "For you."

Carmilla nodded, the smile at her lips growing shy. She whispered, the words as soft as the candle's smoke, "You remembered."

"I try to be accommodating to my friends," I replied, unable to settle the welling pit of *something* inside my stomach at her gaze, a sensation I could not find the word to name.

"Goodnight, dear friend." Carmilla squeezed my hand and left me with a kiss upon my jaw.

I wanted to follow; I wanted to run.

I waited patiently for Carmilla to emerge the next morning at breakfast, and later again at lunch. But she did not emerge until nearly one in the afternoon.

Carmilla came down the stairs on her own accord, meeting me as I left the dining hall from lunch. Across her face spread a beaming, brilliant smile, one I could not help but return. "Laura, my love, what a beautiful day it is."

She made the final few steps, the dark blue of her dress sweeping around her feet. Her hair was done up in curls, and she carried a bonnet in a matching shade to her gown. When she met me, she grabbed my hands and kissed my cheek, as though overjoyed to see me.

"How did you sleep?" I asked, assuming I would someday be used to her strange manner of affection.

"Very well," she replied, and I felt she meant it. Color had returned to her pale cheeks, the palest hint of red. "If you do not mind it, I thought you could give me a tour. I would love to see more of your home. While I do tire quickly in the sun, so long as I rest in the shade every so often, I should have the stamina to go relatively far with no fear."

It seemed a delightful activity, truly. Entranced by her enthusiasm, I said, "Of course. I'll find my father to escort us."

"I would much rather see it through your eyes, my Laura."

On my father's private grounds, we did not need an escort, I supposed. I'd walked by myself a thousand times, but had no wish to impose that upon Carmilla, lest it offend her sensibilities. Instead, I pulled her along toward the door. "My father will have to lead the tour of our home—while I know the layout, he could give you the histories of the art and statues and what the locked rooms were once for. But I have explored the outside since I was old enough to walk."

I opened the door, letting the brilliant sunlight burst into the entry hall. Carmilla visibly cringed as she stole her hand away. She tied the bonnet around her head, though it provided only minimal protection from the sun. "Please, lead the way."

Playing along to her habits, I took her hand myself this time, feeling the rise of some strange excitement in my stomach at her smile. She interlaced her fingers with mine, and I could not say if the sensation were pleasant or nauseating. Nonetheless, I led her across the grassy field toward the nearby grove of fruit trees, knowing she would tire less quickly there.

The sun shone, but a breeze kept the outside world pleasant. Such a sight we were, she in her deep hues of blue and black, myself in pastel pink and white. An aesthetic marvel, as Mademoiselle De Lafontaine might say, her knowledge of art and its history a charming quirk she held.

It reminded me of another artist in my midst. "So, you speak English?" I asked to the girl by my side.

Carmilla nodded, and I slowed my pace to ease her obvious struggle. "And German, French, and a few others."

"How did you come to learn all that? You cannot be much older than I . . ."

Her sudden glower caused my words to falter. "I have sworn to say nothing of my history. And you have promised not to ask."

The stark change in her composure startled me, if only because she seemed to perpetually grin from ear to ear. "I apologize," I said, and her expression softened. "Though I will say it is an odd request of your mother to make."

"My momma is a part of my history."

She was correct, of course. By now, we had reached the trees, and the coolness of the shade descended upon us. Floral scents met my nose, those of the blossoming fruit trees and the green grass at our feet. Had I not felt so shy, I might have taken off my shoes, but instead I helped Carmilla to sit at the base of a tree. She spread her skirts around her like a spring flower, though she herself held the coldness of winter.

I remained standing, self-conscious at her reprimand. "My father inherited all of this from my maternal grandfather," I said instead, gazing about at the shaded copse of trees. Beyond sat a gentle stream, one that fed the lake, glittering in the sunlight even a distance away. "My mother grew up here in Austria, but she met my father on holiday in France. They moved back here upon my grandfather's death, when I was baby."

"So, you are not French?"

Carmilla smiled, amusement on her lip that I couldn't help but match. "I spent many summers in France as a child, visiting my father's family. And it is the native language of my father and all my governesses and so the one I speak best." My smile faltered, afraid to voice my secret insecurity. "I love visiting the towns here, but my failure to speak proper German makes me shy."

"I would be honored to help, if you'll accept it."

So infectious, her charm. "If you wish to bore yourself through Mademoiselle De Lafontaine's lessons, be my guest." I cast my gaze out across the forest floor once more, then pointed beyond the creek. "Up on the hill is the ancient castle where my ancestors once lived, though it is in ruins now, unsalvageable. My father forbade me to ever go without supervision; he fears me running into wolves."

"Would he consider me supervision?" Carmilla's wry grin revealed her jest, yet I could not help but chuckle.

"Doubtful," I replied, and I paced a few steps forward, staring off in the direction of the hill. "It is a fascinating bit of history, however. When your strength is up, I'll ask him to lead us there."

Carmilla's gaze followed me wherever I stepped. "That would be lovely." When she moved to rise, I ran to her side, and she graciously accepted my hand. "My Laura, you are as kind as you are beautiful. Will you show me more?"

I nodded, unsure what to say of her doting. Her mother had proclaimed her sound of mind, yet her words spoke of a specific sort of insanity. Surely she had a suitor back at home, one who clouded her judgement and caused her to speak flowery words of affection. In her haze, she directed such affection at me, for which I could not blame her.

Any alternative spoke of my own insanity.

I led her toward the bank of the stream, watching as she covered her eyes from the water. It reflected the sun's rays, nearly blinding, and so I stood between she and it. Ahead, the cover of trees grew thick again, surrounding an ivy strewn bridge of stone. Another place to sit and rest in the shade, and so I led her forward.

"Are you lonely here, in your castle on the hill?"

Her words pulled me from my musing. Still, her hand rested in mine. "Often," I admitted, and I smiled when I felt her squeeze my fingers.

"So, you are a princess trapped in a tower? Or perhaps a bird in a gilded cage."

I had to laugh at her flowery metaphors. "Neither. My loneliness stems from lack of companionship. I love my home dearly. My father says, should I wish it, I may stay here once I am wed, that my husband and I may fill the deserted halls with children."

"Oh, will you?" she asked, and I felt her suddenly all but fall into my side. I released her hand and held her at the waist, feeling her curl against me. "And who is your suitor, my Laura?"

"Perhaps if I went to town more often, I might have one."

She laughed, and so did I. The thought of a male companion seemed such an odd and foreign thing, some strange and negligible dream I had given little thought to. Should a man wish to pursue me, he would have to dare and climb my tower, as Carmilla had so strangely called it.

I thought to ask her of her own suitors, but I shut my mouth, unwilling to risk her ire yet again. For today, I would let us live in this moment.

"In lieu of a suitor, I shall love you instead," she said, and I heard amusement on her tongue. She kissed me at the side of my lips; oh, how the gesture confused me.

"How can you say you love me? We are of no relation, sweet Carmilla, and we have only met a day ago."

"My darling, you speak such silly things—we met thirteen years ago, and my affection for you has only grown."

Our silent steps upon the grass changed to the gentle clinking of stone as she stepped upon the old bridge. Shaded among the trees, it held a fresh, moist scent, humid and invigorating all at once. Beneath the shade and the hanging leaves, we could not be seen, our own little bubble of time.

"But you are lonely?"

I nodded. Carmilla leaned forward and placed another kiss at my jaw, then released my hands and stepped away, perhaps oblivious to my stiffening form. She rested her elbows upon the stone wall of the bridge, looking down toward the water. A few of her curls escaped her bonnet, framing her face in dark waves.

How lovely she looked, her gentle smile toward the river, the slight breeze tossing the locks of hair upon her head. Yet, there was a sorrow to her features I had not seen before, not since the vision in my childhood.

Unbidden, I placed my hand upon the small of her back, watching as her eyes brightened to match her smile. "I apologize," she whispered. "Sometimes, my thoughts are unbearably loud." I watched her hands, once sitting lightly upon the wall, clench and become one with the stones.

"Carmilla—" Something in my tone must have irked her, for I felt her entire body grow stiff. I removed my hand, watched how her hands grew lax, and felt radiant waves of sorrow seep from the very pores of her skin, it felt. I dearly wished to know her thoughts.

"Perhaps I am not as recovered as I thought," she finally said, curtly, and somehow her tone lacerated the welling discomfort in my stomach, causing it to seep into my limbs. "The sun is stifling. Take me back."

The tension between us mounted, but I could not name it. When I helped her to straighten, she collapsed into my touch, grasping desperately at my collar, her fingers caressing the bare skin of my neck. I saw her eyes grow wide, her full lips become pale and thin. I held her a moment in my embrace, praying, perhaps, that my own health might give her the strength to rise.

"When you saw me in your dream," she whispered, "had you missed me all your life?"

I hesitated, the words burning my lips, for I knew they would wound her vulnerable form. "No," I finally admitted, "but I felt your sorrow as though it were my own. That much, I remember."

And like the vision long ago, I hoped my embrace might be enough to comfort her. I wondered at her thoughts, what strange mystery her life held, and when she moved to pull away, I almost froze to trap her there. Her hand slid from my neck to my chest, pausing at the dip between my breasts.

She clenched her hand, but it gripped beneath my skin and bones. It pained me, her hand wrapping around the tender, beating something beneath it, as though her fingers ruptured holes within my chest, but I could not bear to have her leave.

She released me, and I let her go, frightened at how my heart bled.

On the walk back, she stumbled as she spoke of the sun and the trees, of the beautiful grounds upon which we stood. Her joy had returned, as told by the pleasantries of which she spoke, but though I nodded and responded in time, I understood a deep and terrible thing.

I realized, sinking into my skin like a blanket of snow, how thoughts could grow unbearably loud.

Time passed thusly, of she and I content in each other's presence. We explored the outside, though she took frequent rests within the shade, and soon she could lead as well as follow. And when she had tired sufficiently, we returned to the home. I discovered that she loved to read as well as write, her knowledge of poetry and history remarkable.

In the early afternoon, I found Carmilla seated in the upstairs parlor, her eyes lazily caressing the pages of a book well-beloved of my father. She glanced up at my entrance, her dainty lips pulling into a smile. "I will admit," she said softly, "I find Hugo's commentary on the socio-political climate of the era droll at best, but his writing does captivate me. I could nearly be swayed to believe him." She laughed, as gentle as the streams of sunlight through the window. "Have you read it?"

I shook my head. "Only his poetry."

Carmilla looked back to her book, reciting with a flourish, *"To love or have loved, that is enough. Ask nothing further. There is no other pearl to be found in the dark folds of life."* With a languid sigh, she rested her head upon her hand. "The loveliest sentiment I have ever heard."

"You may be the most romantic person I have ever met," I replied, noting how her eyelashes fluttered. I sat down beside her, and she lounged closer still, smiling as she laid upon my lap, the book held above her face.

Entirely improper, her languor, but living alone in my so-called 'tower,' propriety often fell out the window. Carmilla cast the very aura of serenity, and I wondered if she felt a thrill at the small breaking of etiquette. I busied myself by letting my fingers trace lines through her hair, the gesture relaxing to both of us, as told by the faint, content smile at her lips.

My own mind wandered, but only to idle, passive things, like the texture of her hair and the strange comfort of having a live-in companion. Whatever her oddities, or perhaps because of them, Carmilla's presence uplifted my soul.

My musing was interrupted by the entrance of my governesses. Madam Perrodon stole a glance at Carmilla's book and laughed. "Oh, that depressing thing? Carmilla, have you read it before?"

Carmilla shut the book and said, "A few times, yes."

"You are very well read for a woman of your age," Mademoiselle De Lafontaine chimed, and the two women joined us at the adjacent couch. They made no comment on her lounging, to my relief. I adored the excuse to touch her.

"I have spent enough time ill in bed to have read a library's worth." Carmilla set the book upon her chest, keeping her head cushioned by my lap. "In lieu of travelling, I may adventure at my leisure in the realm of literature. Though I will not lie and say I've never travelled—Hugo's stories of Paris accurately reflect the city."

"You've been to Paris?" Mademoiselle De Lafontaine said, her eyes bright with interest. "It is my birthplace, though I have not been for many years."

Carmilla shut her eyes, reminiscence in her peaceful countenance. "I have a grand affection for the atmosphere of cities. I love the energy."

I could not even fathom such, I realized. Of course, I knew the facts, had read of grand parties and events and rich architecture, but I couldn't imagine the bustle of busy streets.

"As do I." De Lafontaine placed a hand at her chest, palpably excited at the thought. "As a girl, I once attended the *Carnaval de Paris*—I even wore a mask to celebrate. I dreamed of running away and joining an acrobatic troupe with a beloved friend of mine." Her wistful smile spoke of fond memories, the lines of her face growing deep. "Not the life God wanted of me, but I do sometimes wonder what my life would have become."

I withheld a laugh at the visual of De Lafontaine dressed in a rainbow ensemble. Strange, to see the severe woman so at ease, and stranger still to imagine her wanting to join the performers.

"I keep a mask in my bag at all times for such events," Carmilla replied, opening her eyes again. With a wink, she added, "One can never be too prepared for a masquerade."

"You have been to a masquerade?" I asked, heart soaring at the thought.

Carmilla waved off my words. "Oh, a terribly long time ago. I scarcely remember it."

"Carmilla," Madam Perrodon said, quiet until now, "you are hardly old enough to claim you do not remember it."

Carmilla shut her eyes again, serenity settling onto her features. "I suppose I remember a few things. I have attended more than one."

"Have you?" I asked, breathless. I recalled, then, her vow. "Tell us what you can."

She stole my hand, where it lay listless beside her head, and held it in hers, intertwining our fingers. "At my first, I was young—at heart, at least—though old enough to attract attention. I recall the music—*Pachelbel*, if you can believe it—and I know that I danced."

I squeezed her hand, sparing little thought to the warmth in my heart. "I did not know you could dance."

"When I have the stamina, I adore it, my darling," she replied, and I felt as though my governesses had disappeared, and that Carmilla had sucked me into a strange, private world. I imagined Carmilla dressed up for a party, gilded in silk and velvet, donning a crinoline to rival the ballroom walls.

She stiffened in my lap; no one else would have noticed. "I met a man I cared very little for but who cared quite a lot for me."

I heard my heart beat in my ears, heat suddenly bristling against my skin. "Oh?"

"Do not worry yourself," she said, holding tight to my hand. "You will note, I am here with you, and not with him. You will have to fill in the rest of the story yourself; my momma would be furious if she knew I had said any of this."

Such an odd and vexing vow. I wished to know more, to hear of this suitor who Carmilla had apparently slighted.

But the conversation filtered on to lighter things, and Carmilla remained safe in my lap, mine for the moment.

Though I knew not what that meant.

That night, as I sat in my bed, a pen and journal in my hand, a knock startled me from my writing. "Laura?"

I recognized Carmilla's voice. "Come in," I said, and she entered in her graceful way, the lamp reflecting her glowing smile.

She wore only her nightgown, her hair free and flowing, the gold strands within the sea of deep burgundy shimmering in the light. Her eyes held a brightness to them I so rarely saw—it seemed she felt well, this evening.

Carmilla sat at my bedside. "What are you doing?"

"Keeping up with my journal." I blew gently onto the page before shutting it, willing the ink to dry.

Carmilla frowned as I set it aside. "Will you show me?"

Blushing, I shook my head, embarrassed to reveal so much of my soul to anyone.

"No?" She laughed, melodious in her joy. "Why? Too many love poems in my name?"

My blush grew fierce, and still she giggled. "I *do* write of you," I managed to stammer, uncomfortable at the insinuation, though I knew she could not have meant it to embarrass me. "My life has been much more exciting since you came to be in it."

My writing truly was only of her presence and her words. Little of her company. Nothing of my feelings.

I feared what I would find, if I laid my soul bare.

From the pocket of her nightgown, Carmilla withdrew a small object, wrapped in cloth. "I came here to show you something. Do not ask me how I received it, but I thought I ought to show you the source of my musing."

When she unwrapped the cloth, I beheld a gorgeous bit of artwork—a mask bearing silken ties, painted in black and gold. She offered it forward, and I marveled at the work as I held it, noting the etchings of lace in the paste, the light weight. "This absolutely gorgeous."

She plucked it from my hand. The bed shifted as she knelt on the blankets and carefully brought the mask up. She set it against my face. "It suits you," she cooed, the faint whisper of her breath on my ear enough to make me lose my own.

"Does it?"

Her fingers brushed my hair as she stole the mask away, and I nearly didn't notice the wistful smile on her face as she nodded. "Oh, to take you to a ball, my darling Laura! I would love nothing more than to see you dressed up. You would be such a spectacle; I would even do your hair. I know a few things about Parisian fashion."

"You could even teach me to dance," I teased, and she giggled, amused at the notion, it seemed.

"I would be a dreadful teacher."

"Then we would stand as wallflowers," I offered instead, thrilled to see her so full of life, "until some young man came to steal one of us away."

"What use have I for the attentions of men?"

"You met one at your ball, though you slighted him."

I had wanted to push the subject, but the sudden pain in her features suggested I had made some egregious slight. She sat back and began gently wrapping the mask back into its cloth.

"I apologize," I said, daring to steal her wrist. She looked up at me, the forced serenity of her features startling juxtaposed to her normal, easy languor. "I did not mean to—"

"No, Laura, think nothing of it," she said curtly. "But it does vex me when you forget my vow. The time is nearing that you shall know everything, but I dare not anger my momma."

I released her wrist, feeling contrite as I repeated, "I apologize." When her expression remained stagnant, I added, "I only feel as though this remains a great barrier to our friendship—that I may tell you everything but hear nothing of you."

She did not face me now; instead, she looked to the bed. "I can speak of the ball," she whispered. "It is from the time before."

"Before?"

"Before I was ill." In idle motions, she resumed wrapping the delicate mask, her touch as tentative as a butterfly on a flower bud. "I wasn't born to ill health, my Laura. I feel I've spent enough time in bed to mark several lifetimes over, but truthfully, my childhood was sheltered and happy."

She returned the mask to the pocket of her chemise, then met my gaze once more. "I always loved fine things. I remember my dress, thought I was striking in my red and gold. My first ball, and though I was not quite of age to marry, I thought I'd attract every suitor in the state . . ." She smiled, though it held no joy. "I was silly and vain, I flirted like a hussy and recklessly drank, and was later nearly destroyed by a strange . . . *cruel* love that—"

Her words ceased. I saw her tremble; I feared she would cry. "Never mind," she whispered. Her fists tightened, her nails threatening to pierce through her delicate skin. "I will speak no more of it. Not tonight."

Fearful she would hurt herself in her rambling— rambling that suggested a heartbreak I dreaded to know the truth of—I stole one hand into mine, coaxing it to open as I stroked my fingers on her soft skin.

When she relaxed, I repeated the gesture. Her eyes had grown large, her hand shaking in mine. "How are you feeling?" I asked, holding her dainty hand.

"Well enough." She made no move to escape. "I am stronger at night."

Smiling gently, I spared a glance for the window. "Will you walk with me?"

My ploy to see her smile again worked; immediately, she began beaming. "The stars are begging to be admired," she said and as she stood, she pulled me from my bed.

She spoke such poetry. How could I not love her words? I followed her out into the night, speaking of idle, pleasant tidings, her smile brighter than the stars she loved.

Exhaustion tugged at my eyelids as I went down to breakfast. But I was a creature of habit, and though Carmilla and I had not returned until well past midnight, I awoke early and pulled myself from bed.

My father already sat at the table, alone. He smiled at my entrance but worry furrowed his brow. "Good morning, Laura. How are you feeling?"

"Tired. Carmilla and I went for a walk last night, and we returned much later than intended." I sat beside him, and a woman dressed in simple attire immediately hustled in to place a plate before me, filled with delicious scents my sleepless self had no wish for. "But well enough."

As I picked at my plate, exhaustion suppressing my appetite, my father said, "There was a death last night, in the home of one of our servants."

I set the fork down, quite uneasily. "Oh?"

"No warning or sign of sickness, aside from a few days of exhaustion. The girl was fifteen—the picture of health, her mother says. But I've called for the physician to give an exam to anyone the girl was in contact with over the

past few days. She did not work in the house, thankfully."
His concern remained. "Are you certain you are well?"

I nodded. "I will see the doctor, if it will give you
peace of mind, papa. But I swear—after a nap or proper
night's sleep, I will be fine."

"You say you were out with Carmilla?"

I struggled to swallow my first tentative bite.
Pushing the plate away, I said, "I was. Her strength was up,
and she wished to take advantage of her good health and
walk outside."

"I am happy to hear of it," my father said, the first
hints of a smile on his face. "She has been good for you."

"What do you mean?"

He was silent a moment, the graying strands of his
hair apparent in the bright morning light as he looked to
the window. "When your mother passed, I vowed to be
enough for you, to be certain you lacked nothing, even
without your mother's love. You've a calculating mind; you
took to books like most children take to candy. I've tried to
give you everything, but your loneliness was not something
money could fix. I was heartbroken, on both your behalf
and the general's, when Mademoiselle Reinfeldt passed
away, but it seems Carmilla was the miracle you needed.
She has made you smile again."

"She is a wonderful friend," I admitted, yet
uneasiness filled me at the words.

"When her mother returns, I will certainly extend
the offer of hosting the dear girl again—perhaps next
summer, assuming neither you nor she are wed."

Carmilla would someday leave, and my heart could
hardly stand the thought. Was it as my father had said, that
I was truly so unbearably lonely? I recalled Carmilla's
statement, that a gentleman had pursued her at a
masquerade. I had never seen a woman prettier than
Carmilla, and surely others felt the same.

With her romantic heart, surely she had someone
waiting for her. Perhaps she loved him, too. It burned me
to consider it, that she might wed and no longer wish to see
me.

"That would be lovely," I said softly, but my father
frowned again.

"What troubles you?"

I shook my head.

"Laura—"

"I—" I cut off my own words, struggling to articulate my own reservations. "I suppose it simply wounds my heart to think she might wed and forget about me."

My father chuckled, but tenderly he stole my hand. "One does not wed and lose all their friends. If she has a husband, we shall host them both if that would soothe your worried heart." He squeezed my hand, then let it go and whispered, "My fatherly heart would rather forget it, but you are of age to be married. I hope you will keep your mind open to any suitors who come to call."

"Suitors?" I scoffed. "I do not know any men, much less any who would come to woo me."

He hesitated a moment too long.

My good humor faded. "Who?"

"My Laura, it is not something to trouble yourself with—"

"You would not have brought this up without cause."

My father's hands grasped each other above the table. "Nothing has been decided. I would allow no one to decide your fate but you, my Laura, but there is a man with whom I have been in correspondence who I know to be honorable and good. And I am to say no more than that until he—"

"Do I even know him?" I asked, the reality of my changing future steadily settling into my skin, causing it to grow ice cold. "I do not know any available men, Papa, and I cannot marry someone I have not even met."

"You have met him."

"But then who—" My words stopped all at once, realization settling in with reality. I brought my hand from my chest to my mouth, my lungs suddenly frozen. "General Spielsdorf?"

With a resigned sigh, my father nodded. "It was the purpose of he and Bertha's visit. Bertha, you would have learned, was soon to be wed and leave him for Paris in the upcoming months, and so I proposed he consider—"

"*You* proposed it?" The words felt like a betrayal. "Papa, he is old."

"He is younger than me, and Laura, I will not be around forever."

I knew he was right. My father's failing health would someday steal him from me. Still, time suddenly seemed too fast; the bubble of stagnation popped, thrusting me forward.

"He is a widower," my father continued, his voice softer now. "His wife passed away giving birth to their first child, who died not days later. Bertha was his niece whom he took into his home when his sister passed away shortly after her birth. Laura, he is a kind man and would be a wonderful father to your children."

It was as blessed a life as any woman could ask for.

"If you tell him no, I will respect your decision," my father said. "You are wise beyond your years, in so many ways. But I would request you give him a chance to present himself."

I nodded, my whole being unsettled at the words. Forcing a smile, I stood from the table. "I will consider it, I swear," I whispered, and I left him, leaving behind my full plate of food.

He did not stop me.

I spoke of it to no one—not until that afternoon, when Carmilla inquired after my mood.

"Laura, darling, you have been unusually quiet, even for you."

She sat at the base of a tree within the grove near my father's house. With the wind gently brushing my hair, the crisp air awakening my senses, it should have been a joyous day—what with company and the promise of beautiful weather.

But Carmilla knew me, at least well enough for this. "If I tell you, you must keep it secret," I whispered, letting it filter into the breeze.

A frown marred her lovely face. She beckoned me downward, and so I sat, mindful of the grass that might stain my pastel dress. Her hand reached up to cup my face, bringing me close. Her thumb caressed my cheek. "You may tell me anything."

"There is a gentleman who will soon be calling for me," I said, acutely aware of the pout of her pretty lips, "in a manner of speaking."

Carmilla's dark eyes widened to match her frown. "You have a suitor?"

"I do." I looked down to her lap, my face still cupped by her hand. "And my father reminded me of his own mortality and has encouraged me to consider the eminent proposal."

I had witnessed Carmilla's ever-shifting dramatics before—her spirited gestures, her overly-familiar affections, even her odd near-flirtation. But never had I seen her look utterly sober.

"Do you want to be married to him?"

"I do not know," I replied. "I have never thought of marriage, like I said before."

Her hand fell away, the warmth lingering against my cheek. "When will he be coming?"

"I do not know precisely, but a few more weeks."

She was quiet a moment—so damnably, uncharacteristically quiet—and when I thought she might have turned to stone, her visage changed into a cheery smile. "As I said before," she said, the hint of a laugh on her throat, "in lieu of a suitor, I shall love you instead—much more than your gentleman caller ever could."

And so returned her oddness. I could not say if I had missed it. I thought to protest. "Carmilla—"

But her laughter stole my words. She leaned over and planted a kiss upon my cheek, pulling heat to my fair skin. Her laughter only escalated. "How pretty you look when you blush," she teased.

Some insanity overtook me, because I immediately leaned over and kissed her back—on the hollow of her cheek.

In that half a moment, hardly a breath of time, my lips felt the softness of her cheek, the smooth skin unmarred by facial hair. Though I certainly imagined it, I thought I felt blood rise to the surface, for when I pulled away there was a blush.

And I felt, unquestionably, a surge of excitement course through my blood. It lit every nerve within my body, settling just as quickly at the base of my abdomen. The temptation for something I could not even name drove me to eye her lips as though they were some delectable dessert—for I wanted so badly to know what they tasted of.

Instead, I pulled away and forced a smile, refusing to dwell on how adorable surprise looked on her beautiful face. Carmilla's shock settled into an embarrassed grin, and I wondered if I had finally outwitted her in her own game.

Unwilling to speak, I steadily fell back and laid upon the cool grass, wondering, not for the first time, how thoughts could grow unbearably loud.

A slight weight settled at the juncture between my shoulder and my breast. Carmilla's hair tickled my mouth as she whispered, "Do you mind? I feel . . ." I felt her sigh against me, her arm falling around my waist. ". . . so very tired."

"Please stay," I replied, surprised at my own desperate tone. But I wanted her here, to stay, because all was well, all was well, all was well . . .

Time stood still. I clung to it with all my might.

But when the shadows shifted, when the sun beamed down onto my face, I felt it jostle and move again, like some ancient machine unwillingly forced to start.

In the evening, I searched for her after dinner—she had been absent, her appetite as fickle as the wind. My shoes were quiet upon the stone floor, the shyness of my childhood teaching me to creep like a mouse through my father's home. Countless rooms, most locked from disuse, passed me by, but the décor of the hallway glistened in the fading light.

A gaggle of giggling servant girls gossiped from behind the open door of a storage closet. ". . . claims she's tired all the time and cannot work. Says she has nightmares of some demon."

"I hear she's been lifting her skirts a few too many times for the gardener. Perhaps it finally caught up to—"

The women looked startled at my passing, watching me like a doe appearing from the forest. Were my appearances truly so rare? I passed them by, a silent ghost haunting my own home.

Great double doors led to a room never used, not in my nineteen years of living. I was surprised to see one slightly ajar. With trepidation, though I already suspected the truth, I peeked within.

A sole figure stood within the grand ballroom, perfectly centered beneath the chandelier. The sunset illuminated the rich décor through enormous windows dotting the western wall and, cast in shadows of orange and gold, Carmilla admired the cloth-covered statues and unlit candelabras upon the wall. Glittering lights from the glass chandelier, refracted from the fading sun, burst across the floor. She stood among a sea of stars, her skin celestial and alight.

I stepped inside; she turned at my entrance. "I hadn't the honor of seeing this room during your father's tour of his home. Absolutely spectacular." She continued her turn, twirling as though dancing, her gown sweeping around her feet. "And you've never been to a ball, you say?"

I shut the door and shook my head as I approached. "I've never seen this room in use. When my father and mother were engaged, my grandfather threw an engagement party and invited the entire countryside. But that was the last time it was used." I let my next words mull about my mouth, nearly choking on them before they escaped. "Perhaps the next time will be my own."

Carmilla stole my hands when I approached, both of us glittering beneath a rainbow of glass. "To your general?"

Horrified, I shushed her. "No one is to know that. Everyone gossips here. My father would be furious if the news came back to him."

There was a wickedness to her grin that made my blood race. She placed my hand on her shoulder, and then her own at my waist. "The waltz is back in fashion. I am an

42

atrocious teacher, but I can at least teach you to count in threes."

She did—tried to, at least, my feet stumbling while hers were light. Though weakness drove her languid motions, she led as well as she could, a gentleman in masquerade.

I wondered, were she a gentleman, if my increasing affection for her would be the same.

In steps of three, but in a square, I shambled along. After a few too many stumbled and scattered apologies, I said, "You must think me so droll."

"Whatever do you mean, my darling?" We stopped our steps, simply swaying now upon the stone floor, beneath the sea of lights.

"I cannot dance, much less walk like a proper lady, but even underneath your illness, you have so much grace in your steps. And look at you—" I did so, admiring the brocade of her silken gown, the dark sea of her hair as it fell in perfectly pinned ringlets. ". . . you said yourself you love the energy of cities. You know fashion and parties better than I ever could. I feel like a silly country girl standing next to you."

Our bodies touched, though my skirts and corset prevented me from feeling her. A terrible cage, keeping us apart—

By God—that was dangerous thinking.

I might've stumbled back for shock, but Carmilla held me gently enthralled. "You are perfect, my darling. You're perfect, and you are mine. I could never think less of you."

She thought the world of me, and I felt like a wolf romancing a lamb. "You hardly know me."

"I told you—we met thirteen years ago. That nearly makes me your oldest friend." Carmilla's blush blossomed in tandem with the light fading from the window. Drenched in darkness, she whispered, "Not a silly country girl—a princess in a tower."

I saw nothing, merely felt her hand in mine, the slight pressure of her other on my waist. Our steps had stopped—we simply held each other in the dark. "Your romanticism puts poets to shame," I whispered back, my other senses alight in lieu of my missing sight.

I heard her chuckle, girlish and sweet. "But aren't you the poet, my Laura? You and your secret writings." She took her hand off my waist; instead, it burned my neck as she caressed her fingers along the curve.

Nervous, I reach up and clutched her hand, gently pulling it away. "We should go—I scare in the dark—"

"The dark?" Her laughter shouldn't have intoxicated me so. "Darling, darling, the dark has never hurt a soul. Perhaps be more concerned for its inhabitants."

If the words were meant to set me at ease, she failed. But her laughter lightened our path as she escorted me to the hallway.

After a week's time, I discovered how far Carmilla's romanticism went.

For my nineteenth birthday, I had received a collection of Shakespearean works from my father. Carmilla awoke late every morning, though she often retired early, and so although it was noon I had no reason to expect her approach.

In the upstairs parlor, I sat, the cadence of Shakespearean English becoming a pattern in my head, when a sudden hint of breath by my ear caused my heart to start. Hands slowly slid down my shoulders from behind, and when I turned my head, I saw Carmilla leaning over me. "*These violent delights have violent ends*," she whispered, reading the text on the page. I felt her lips smile against my ear. "*And in their triumph die, like fire and powder, which, as they kiss, consume.*" She pulled away, sighing as though in ecstasy, and came around to sit beside me on the couch. "Can you imagine sweeter words, my Laura?"

"Sweeter words than those describing a love doomed for tragedy?" I asked, unable to help my incredulous tone. Perhaps she had not read this one.

"A tragedy, perhaps, but to think of how they lived—the passion they shared! Oh, to die, nay—to die together, so that we may live together!" Her head fell back upon the couch, hand resting at her heart.

"You speak as one in the very fires of love," I said, and I hoped my sardonic humor did not convey too strongly. I teased her, perhaps cruelly, but she looked at me with all the devotion of the foolish lovers in my book.

Carmilla leaned in close, pursing her lips in a matter to make my heart flutter. "You say you would not die for me?"

"Carmilla, we are not lovers," I said, astonished at my own defensive tone.

She merely laughed at my words. "Darling, you cannot say you do not love me."

"I *do* love you, Carmilla. I care for you very much." Her words made me cross, expanded the perpetual pit in my stomach until it threatened to burst and consume me whole. I prayed she would leave and take her incessant teasing with her.

"And, my Laura, you must know I love you more dearly than I have ever loved another. So what are we but caught in a perfect love affair—"

"Carmilla, we are not—" I stopped myself, fearing my own fury. Despite her strange and sometimes irksome quirks, she did not deserve my wrath. "To be lovers implies we have . . ." I stopped, demure at the words, my own innocence apparent as I squashed down the unease in my throat. The book seemed much easier to stare at than Carmilla's coquettish gaze. ". . . it implies we have made love, and for two women, that would be quite impossible."

She said absolutely nothing. When I finally dared to meet her stare, her eyebrow had lifted, as though a challenge had been issued. Heat filled my cheeks at the stare, dangerous and sensuous all at once. Carmilla crept forward like a cat stalking prey. "My darling, history tells of centuries of women loving women in all manner of beautiful ways. With their hands, with their tongues—no man can know a woman as another woman can. Have you not read of Greece? Of the history of Sappho and the lovers she kept?" Our knees touched, then to my horror she lifted one and straddled my lap. With her slight chest a mere breath away from my mouth, Carmilla gazed down and recited, *"You may forget, but let me tell you this—"*

"Carmilla, please!" I shouted, the pressure in my chest too much, too soon. She removed herself; I tore away from the couch. "Your games are vexing; I beg you to stop!"

All semblance of passion faded from her countenance. Carmilla appeared as nothing more than a frightened kitten. "I play no games—"

"This flirtation must end!" Her pain wounded me, shredded my heart in ways I dared not confront. "Even in jest, what you tease of is wrong. What if my father heard you speak? By God—what if he'd seen?"

Carmilla sat as a wounded animal upon the couch, hands trembling, skittish and broken. Her wide eyes bespoke the coming of tears. "I—" She cut off her words, tearing her gaze away as she brought her arms up to cover her face.

I ran from her. My heart yearned to comfort her, and so I ran, unwilling to break from my stance. To my bedroom, and there I shut the door, sliding down the heavy wood and collapsing upon the polished, stone floor.

Oh, I cursed my tears! My heart shattered in ways I dared not confront, the welling pit in my stomach growing ever deeper. The brewing heat between my legs frightened me more than the tantalizing implications of Carmilla's cursed words—for as much as I hated what she said, as much as it spat in the face of the convictions ingrained in me from my birth, I longed to know more, to bathe in those sensuous words. Yes, I knew of Greece, of islands of woman devoted to ungodly passions; I also knew of witches burned at the stake.

If this were love, I wished it dead. My will was nothing to hers, I feared. But her will was nothing to God's.

When I emerged from my bedroom, my face had long ago stopped swelling. I had run out of tears in time, fear and loathing replaced with an empty shell, a barricade against the ever-present waves of emotion sloshing against my rocky resolve.

I feared, in my panic, that I had made an awful mistake, accused a woman with no ill-intent of a heinous crime. Had I projected my own insecurity—my own personal temptation—onto sweet Carmilla? The virulent storm of my own making merely that—only mine?

The sun still shone out my window as my feet stepped through the rich hallways. To my surprise, I heard laughter from downstairs and ran to investigate.

I found them in the drawing room—Carmilla and my governesses. I could hardly understand the words my friend spoke, nor any of them as they rapidly spat out phrases in German.

"Oh, come join us, Laura," Mademoiselle De Lafontaine said upon my entrance. "Carmilla's German is excellent, for a woman born in France."

"Or so we assume," Perrodon added with a wink in Carmilla's direction. "She is content to keep her secrets."

I shook my head, my eyes transfixed on Carmilla, who in turn seemed frozen to me. Her apparent amusement had faded, wide eyes conveying some muted shame. "I am not surprised," I replied, forcing myself to step toward her. "She is a well-versed woman. I think she may appreciate poetry even more than I do."

I stole her into my arms, feeling her stiffen and then collapse. To those who watched, it would be nothing more than an overly friendly gesture of welcome, but to Carmilla it meant the affirmation of some deep, abiding truth—that I cared for her still.

Though for me, it confirmed what I feared: that I adored her presence, that my heart soared at our touch. But for the sake of our friendship, and for the sake of her tender heart, I set that aside.

She pulled away without any excess displays of affection—no kisses upon my jaw, no lingering caress on my cheek or my waist, and I found I missed it dearly.

I sat beside her on the couch, joining in the cacophonous banter, though I struggled to keep up, my German lacking at best. I marveled at Carmilla's gift of tongues, how her smooth voice made even the harsh consonants sound almost musical.

Thus continued the afternoon, until my father entered, a somber expression on his face. "I apologize for dampening the mood, but there is news. Perhaps you recall Mademoiselle Annette Charon?"

I did, and I told him such. "We played in the garden together, as children. I recall that she was dear to me."

"We've received word of her passing," my father said, his countenance conveying regret. "Her funeral shall be held in three days' time, and we are invited."

My heart sunk. It had been a decade or more since we had played together, though when in town we often met. I did not cry, no, but it felt as though some weight had fallen upon my vision, turning it into shades of blue and gray. "But she was so young! Oh, her poor father," I said, and upon my arm, Carmilla's hand gently came to rest. "What was the cause of death?"

"The letter did not say. Perhaps the service will answer the question for us."

He joined us in the drawing room, speaking a moment of poor Annette, but we let the conversation drift to pleasant things, as false and heavy as it felt.

The weighty mood carried into the next day, and so my father, perhaps sensing this, proclaimed that we should all be enlisted in a project.

It was servants' work, his plot, but I appreciated the sentiment behind it—we would go to the attic and sift through the antique treasures awaiting us there. Some would be kept—family heirlooms and such—but others, he insisted, we give away, for the sake of space and of tarnishing their worth.

We began upon Carmilla's awakening, near late afternoon—and oh, the poor girl seemed exhausted. I had bid her goodnight early, unwilling to jostle what remained of the morass in my chest, but I did not know when she decided to sleep. I asked her, "Are you certain you have the strength to join us? I worry the dust will irritate your lungs."

Carmilla smiled, soft and sincere. I suppressed how it made my heart flutter and fly. "Your worry for my health is appreciated, my Laura. But I will be fine; I swear it."

And so she joined us—my father, my governesses, and I.

"Oh, look at this, Laura," De Lafontaine proclaimed amidst the calamitous work. She held up a tarnished locket, and when she handed it to me, it bore the visages of two people inside. "It is the wedding portraits of your grandparents—absolutely stunning!"

The attic sprawled wide, windows letting filtered sunlight in to illuminate the room. Servants had cleared the area of cobwebs and dust as well as they could, but I wore an older dress nonetheless, one I cared not if it tore or stained. The ceiling arched high, slanted for support, and we each sequestered ourselves in our own private corner, though Carmilla kept near to mine.

I tucked the locket into my pocket. "It ought to be displayed," I replied. "Perhaps in the parlor, with the other family portraits."

I returned to the box of lace I had been investigating, stitched by some unknown ancestor long ago. Such a waste, I thought, to keep it hidden up in here—it ought to be displayed on the sleeves of a fine gown.

I glanced over to Carmilla, whose dainty hands gently glossed upon an ancient trunk, and wondered how lovely the lace might look sewn onto the ends of her black sleeves—add a bit of friendliness to her cold aura.

From the corner, my father suddenly stiffened. I watched him tilt his head, staring in wonder at some portrait amidst a bundle. "Laura, Carmilla—you must see this." We approached, and he continued with, "It is dated for 1698."

He held up the portrait in question, and my own eyebrows threatened to fly from my face. A beautiful portrait, faded from age and the onslaught of air, but it bore an unmistakable likeness—to that of Carmilla herself!

But Carmilla gave an easy laugh—languid, always languid, even in her excitement. "Well, would you look at that! We even share the mole upon my neck."

They did, I was startled to realize.

"Oh, tell me the title," she continued. "Does it bear one?"

My father searched the back, then said, "It appears to be the painting of one Countess Mircalla Karnstein. Mircalla is not a name in my lineage, but my late wife's mother's maiden name was Karnstein."

Again, Carmilla laughed, more delighted than before as she clapped her hands. "It is a name in mine as well! Perhaps she is some progenitor of ours."

I took the portrait from my father's hands—it was no larger than a journal. "May I have it, papa? I'll keep it safe, perhaps stow it in my bedside table."

My father nodded, and smiling, said, "It will make a wonderful keepsake of our dearest guest when she finally has to leave us."

I hadn't considered that. In a few months' time, Carmilla would leave. My heart felt relieved yet wounded beyond recognition.

When the sun began to set, the attic grew dark, and so we proclaimed ourselves done for the day. My father's plot had succeeded—we were all in lighter spirits, even myself.

I did as I said and went to place the portrait of the late countess in my bedside table, when soft steps alerted me to her presence—Carmilla stood in the doorway. "I feel so stifled after spending all day inside. Will you come walk with me? I do so love the night."

The sun had set. I looked out my window and saw the full moon shining silver streaks across my bed. "I would be happy to."

I followed her out into the night.

From the house we stepped across the stone path, toward the grove of trees my father kept. Bathed in moonlight, Carmilla's skin turned luminous, glowing, and I swore in that moment she was no mere manifestation of flesh and blood but of another creed; something holy, some angel with whom I was blessed to be acquainted. Her dark hair swept in easy sheets of burgundy and gold, left to fall loose behind her nightgown and robe.

It seemed I had fallen behind; Carmilla laughed as she beckoned me forward. I took her hand, so soft and slight, and let her lead me into the copse of trees.

She seemed energized beneath the night sky, livelier than I had ever seen. With a smile as gentle as the morning dew, Carmilla teased, "You would keep the portrait of my likeness? Of my ancestor, Countess Mircalla?"

I felt the first blossoming of heat against my cheeks. "She bears the countenance of someone dear to me," I said, and she pulled me forward into her arms and set her hands at my waist.

The tenderness of the intimate gesture pierced through the wall I had hastily constructed around my heart. "And keep her by your bedside?" she said, a glint of mischief in her eye.

"Safest there," I replied, and so came the rise of that unnatural thing within me, the heat I had no words to name. I could not express what her stare did to me, only that it brought a welling of shame, a wrongness that spat in the face of my upbringing.

And with it, something I craved. I could not step away. I grew weaker with every passing moment.

Instead, Carmilla's touch left the curve of my waist. She smiled. I missed her presence. "My family line is an ancient one. I have it written back a thousand years."

"But you'll tell me nothing more?" I asked, but immediately regretted the words. Carmilla's frown was one I'd seen before, that same glower whenever I pushed her for details of her life, of her mother's quest. Yet desperation to know more of this mysterious young woman pushed me to act; I could have bathed in every piece of her, but I was left parched for thirst.

"I have made a vow, my darling Laura," she said with some regret. "But I swear, in time, you will know all things." Her smile returned. She stole my hand and pulled me along, deeper into the collection of trees and shrubs.

She moved with the smoothness of a cat, and with the same sort of odd flirtation. We always touched; she always caressed my hand, my waist, my face, the sighs leaving her mouth reminiscent of a purr. I could have sworn she were a gentleman in masquerade for how she gazed at me, adoration in her eyes.

And I wondered, if she were, if this would be a different sort of meeting. I wondered if I'd love her the same.

Whatever amorous passions drove her touch and smile, it spoke of someone in a haze of romantic entanglement. I had thought as much before, and the oddly desperate urge to know, the morass within my chest, drove me to cross my self-imposed line. I asked, "Perhaps I can guess."

She turned, keeping my hand enthralled, the coy twisting of her lip nothing less than girlish. She was no masquerading gentleman; not with the stark femininity of her laughter. Oh, Carmilla, so soft and bright in the filtered moonlight! "Tell me," she said, a challenge in her voice. "Tell me of me, my Laura. I love to hear you speak."

"You come from a land far away," I said, but she laughed and shook her head. "No?"

"No," she whispered, and she stepped in quite close, enough for me to count every individual lash of her fluttering eyes.

I momentarily lost my words, so adoring was her gaze. My stomach churned at her closeness, yet within me something begged for more. "Not so far, then. You come from money."

She gave a slight nod, the mischief in her smile fading into something unfathomably soft.

This ineffable swelling in my chest threatened to burst, and yet my heart still accommodated every strange and wonderful feeling. I remained repulsed yet enticed, knowing not what I dared to ask for. "Your father has passed away."

Again, she nodded. Her hand left mine and instead settled on my waist. Her fingers skimmed the fabric of my nightgown, thin enough that my skin felt bare beneath her hands.

We stood level to each other, for though she was slight she was not small. The gentleness in her stare brought, again, thoughts of lovers and romance. "At home, there is a young man you love. He waits for you."

Her gaze remained the same, even as she slowly shook her head.

"No?"

Carmilla pursed her lips ever so slightly, and I wondered a moment at their softness. "I have been in love with no one." One hand left my waist and instead slid oh so lightly against my neck, settling to cup my cheek. She so often had, the intimacy of it both jarring and lovely all at once. But here and now, with the speckles of moonlight from the trees against her fair skin, with the breeze in her hair and the closeness of her breath, it frightened me so. "And I shall never be in love with anyone, I think," she continued, and then she leaned in and whispered, "unless it be with you."

Her lips touched mine. With the gentleness of butterflies upon petals, we kissed beneath the grove of trees, secluded from the world, lost in time. My hands settled at her hips, drawn in by her languid motions, and when her mouth parted for her tongue, the joy in my heart threatened to burst. Some noise escaped my throat, like a soft cry of pain, and with it came the welling of a temptation I feared to name.

It frightened me so, and when she pulled away, the tenderness in Carmilla's gaze shook me to my very soul. I withheld a sob for the shame that rose within me, the pleasure I felt in her amorous touch. My body and heart cried for more, longing to bask in her presence, but I knew—*I knew*—it was wrong.

Carmilla's eyes spoke not of friendship, no, but of passion and light. I thought of the women who wrote poetry of their own affection for women, whose lives were a tragedy, meant for heartbreak in the arms of men or a pyre of hellish flame.

Fearing tears, I drew away, though it stole what little willpower I still held. She stepped forward to follow. "Carmilla, we should not—we *cannot*—"

Oh, how *beautiful* she looked in the moonlight.

Perhaps it was weakness, yet euphoria filled me as I fell again into her arms, my lips stealing hers with a desperation she returned. This time, I heard her moan as her body pressed against a tree. My inexperience was outmatched by desire, I hoped, but her lips knew the motions, of how to kiss and leave me utterly breathless. I had felt nothing like it in my nineteen years, living in a pocket of innocence, untouched by passion of any creed.

When I pulled away, I saw her smitten demeanor, her desperation to be consumed utterly as she gazed at me with radiant joy. "Laura—"

My own name pulled me back into the world. I stepped back, cutting off her words. "Y-You look frail, Carmilla," I said, unsteady as I stumbled across the words I had to say to run. "We should return."

"I feel perfectly fine—"

"Carmilla, I need—" I cut myself off, resisting the urge to sob. "I have to go. I need . . . I need time."

The seconds grew long, tension mounting. I saw her joy dangle by a single, taut string, one I held the knife to sever.

"Let us go back," she finally whispered, her tone unsteady. She kept her hands to herself as she stepped away.

With the manor soon in sight, I followed her through the grass and trees.

Chapter Two

That night, I began to dream. For if it remained a dream, it could not be a sin.

I lay in my bed, kept awake by the memory of Carmilla's kiss on my lips, when a weight at the foot of my bed pulled me from my semi-conscious state. There she knelt, dressed in white, innocence in her gaze. Silently, she came forward, and when she caught my eye she smiled.

She held a finger to my lips, imploring me to hush. Then, she kissed my lips again, and my body rejoiced at our reunion. Carmilla caressed my neck, steadily trailing her kisses down to match, her lips lightly sucking upon my skin. She settled below the collar of my nightgown, and I withheld a gasp when I felt the sting of her bite.

But her hands continued downward, fingers skimming the thin fabric of my chemise. She cupped my breasts, my vestal form alight at every touch. Soon she left my chest, smiling with unspeakable warmth, adoration in her dark eyes. I thought to ask what spell she concocted, if it were witchcraft or a prayer to God, but then she placed her head between my thighs and kissed until my soul left my body.

When I awoke, she had vanished, no sign of her presence save for the mark on my chest, one I hid behind the high collar of my dress. Some ineffable piece of me had gone, rewritten by her touch, and what had been stolen was patched by a piece of her, some bit of her heart I had unknowingly taken with me.

We spoke nothing of it save for passing glances in the afternoon, yet she moved as though nothing had changed. And nothing had—she remained a vivacious flirt, holding my hand wherever we went, offering to braid and style my golden hair. Carmilla did as she had always done.

And yet everything had changed, the way she walked utterly enthralling to my gaze, the charm in her words pulling easy laughter from my throat. It scared me so, this dream we shared. What transpired last night had been nothing more than a passionate vision, something unspeakable, yet unspeakably warm.

That night, I dreamed she moved within me. She spoke my name—*"Darling, darling . . . Laura, how I love you so."*— and when she withdrew, I sobbed. We were one; I prayed she'd stay.

Unbidden, in my haze, I addressed her: "Carmilla, what does this mean?"

She placed a kiss upon my brow. "Sleep, my love," she whispered. "This world was not made for lovers such as us. But do not fear; instead, we shall build our own."

I gripped her dress as she turned to leave, pulling her back into my arms. She acquiesced, falling into my embrace. "Laura—"

"Please, stay," I begged through tears. I felt her shift and settle into the plush sea of blankets. My mouth sought hers, our lips touching with all the passion of our apparent love affair. What had settled within me began to simmer anew, and this time, I dared to touch Carmilla—*my* Carmilla—beneath her nightgown, reveling in every sigh from her lips. First with my hands and then my mouth, I chartered a map of her body, detailing every curve and line.

All the voices in my head, the ones that screamed *abomination*, grew silent when we moved as one, myself and my Carmilla. Naked beneath me, she cried in ecstasy, and again I felt complete. Two halves of a whole, she and I, and by God I understood—I felt I had missed her all my life.

Later, we lay entangled in each other's arms, naked and free and yet enslaved all at once. For I was bound to her by a force far stronger than any chain—by gentle strands of light, our hearts had woven together.

And so I told her, the words fluttering from my lips delicate and damning all at once. "I love you, Carmilla."

She kissed me tenderly. A beautiful thing, to be cherished by her. "And you know I love you, my Laura." Camilla held me to her breasts, and I breathed in her scent, allowing my heartbeat to steady and soothe.

My vision ended. I awoke to streams of sunlight across my pillow.

Exhausted from dreaming, I laid in a stasis upon my bed until a knock on my door startled me. "Laura?" My father's voice met my ear. "Are you feeling all right?"

The handle turned. In a panic, I hid myself beneath the covers, unwilling to answer any questions regarding my nudity. Only my head peeked out when my father opened the door. "I hardly slept," I admitted, and to even implicate myself aloud caused a jolt of panic to course through my veins.

"Are you well enough to come to Mademoiselle Annette's funeral?"

"I am. But leave me alone to dress first."

He nodded. "I will inform Madam Perrodon that you've awoken. Rouse Carmilla, if you think she might enjoy an excursion into town. A pity we must go for such a somber affair, but perhaps the outdoors might do the girl some good."

He left me alone.

Guilt steadily welled in the hollow of my stomach. All that remained was my nakedness and the mark upon my neck, bruised beneath Carmilla's mouth once more, yet the reality of my crimes settled upon my heart. Yesterday, I had lived in absolute overwhelm, not quite denial but . . . as though it were some mystery for my mind to unravel.

Now, it lay scattered before me, the forsaking of my chastity. Tears welled in my eyes, the calm before the storm that shook me to my core. I wept upon my bed, the image of her erotic form burned behind my eyelids, my fingers craving the writings they had felt within her. Oh, my Carmilla—heartbreak remained our inevitable end, either in utter ruin from our families or upon our deaths in Hell's great flame.

Perhaps my soul was damned already, having succumbed to her touch. My weakness lay apparent, the temptation of her love too much for me to bear.

A knock startled me. "A moment, please." My eyes had surely swollen, but I stood from my bed nonetheless and threw on my chemise, unwilling to explain my nakedness. I opened the door, unsurprised to see my governess.

"Heavens, child," Perrodon said, scooping me up into her arms. "What has happened?"

"Heartbroken for Annette," I lied, scarcely feeling her crushing embrace. Her kind smile told me she understood.

She helped me assemble muted shades of black and gray. I rarely wore such subdued palettes, but my heart hung as heavy as the weight of the inevitable funeral party.

"Laura, what is that?"

As I adjusted the skirts at my waist, I followed her gaze—to the blossoming mark from Carmilla's teeth. It peeked just above the neckline of my chemise, and I recoiled as I brushed against it, surprised at how tender the bruising remained. "Must've poked it, somehow."

She said nothing more, instead helping to cinch me into my clothing. When she finished, I steeled my resolve as I dabbed at my tears. My swollen eyes had settled, red from what I could explain away to anyone else as exhaustion. "I'll awaken Carmilla," I whispered, daunted at the thought. "She scares so easily."

When I left my room, my shoes echoed across the deserted halls like gunshots through a silent night.

Carmilla's door stood as an impenetrable force, some monster I had no weapon to slay. I feared, in the depths of my self-loathing, that I might someday come to hate her, but the thought seemed unfathomable now. Knowing her propensity to startle, I said, "Carmilla?" and then I knocked against the heavy wood.

It was early for her to awaken, but she had been reminded the evening prior—hopefully she remembered.

From within, I heard gentle rustling, soft steps upon the floor. I braced myself, then watched as her face appeared between the crack of the door and its frame.

"Good morning," I said, unable to stifle my smile. Oh, my Carmilla—*my Carmilla*—what spell had she cast upon me?

Her own lip twisted to match, her tired eyes lightly blinking. "My dearest Laura—good morning," she said, for she always spoke in flowery words, even though it tore through every wall I could construct. "Will you help me decide my funeral dress?"

Unbidden, I nodded, then followed her in, trembling when she locked the door behind us.

Her nightgown fell to the floor, and of course I took her for my own, of course I kissed the bitterness between her legs. Her quiet moans sang like music, the sweetest love song, one I joined as a duet as I whispered her name—*"Oh, Carmilla, Carmilla, my love, my heart . . ."*

When she had fallen back to earth, she pushed herself up with shaking limbs and fell into my embrace. We had not spoken of this—not truly, other than my plea of last night—and now was not the time. I feared to speak of it, to name the sin, face it like the beast it was, but for me to understand we would need to convene.

But not now, not with our eminent departure. Not when the sunlight shone so lively through the window. Instead, as I gazed down to her face pressed against my clothed chest, I saw her contentment, utter peace upon her countenance.

And that shook me deeper than my sin, for her joy remained a radiant thing.

Wordlessly, I helped her to dress, my skin alight at every touch upon her form. Chaste, yet sensuous, helping to cinch her corset, preen and primp her hair.

"So, you are always so quiet."

Her teasing startled me. She turned to me, a coy smile at her lips. "Tell me your thoughts," she continued. "We have spoken of nothing since . . ." Her smile turned shy, tenderness shining in the liquid dark of her eyes. "Well, you have been very reserved, yesterday and today."

Those damning words. I feared what I might say. My hands fell to my side, and perhaps she sensed the change in my demeanor. Her smile faded, and she gently stole my hands into her smaller ones, interlacing our fingers as she gazed at me. "Laura, please say something."

Carmilla's soothing words broke me, and again I fell into tears. She released my hands and pulled me against her body, pressing my head lightly into her shoulder where I sobbed. Wetness stain her dress, but I could not seem to stop.

I felt her hand draw words of comfort against my hair. Finally, I managed to say, "I am so frightened."

"Frightened of what, my darling?"

"Of *this!*" I exclaimed. I pulled away, trembling as I held my hands against my chest. "Of these feelings I have, of your touch, of the spell you've apparently cast on my heart. I am petrified of being found out, yet I do not even have the words to name what this is."

Carmilla said softly, "This is love. This is you and me, together—"

"Carmilla, we cannot—" My own sob cut off my words. "What future do we have?"

"Let me worry for the future, my love—"

"I beg of you—stop with your poisonous words of affection! I do not know even now if you are sincere!" Oh, the remark was cruel, and the light gasp she gave told me I had wounded her deeply. But I meant it, though I hated to say it, for her flirtation remained as it had since the first day we met. "Do you love me, Carmilla? Or do you merely toy with me for your entertainment?"

Carmilla cast her gaze to the floor. Her hands wrenched up to cover her face, and I heard her tremulous gasp, watched her fight her inevitable sobs. I resisted the urge to go to her, merely watched like some cruel taskmaster as she fought to keep composure.

She turned around, then crumpled to the floor.

Fearing her health, I fell beside her, hesitant as my hand settled onto her back. I felt her flinch. Then, I heard her whisper, "I love you desperately."

My fist clenched against her back. My own jaw began trembling. "Carmilla, I've spoken out of turn," I replied, and I felt panic course through my blood as she curled into a tight ball, hiding her face. "I am so sorry. I love you, and that frightens me so."

I felt her quiver beneath my hand. I let it slide around, holding her in an awkward embrace as I brought the other up to try and coax her arm away from her face. My fingers brushed the damp sleeve of her black dress. "Carmilla, please—"

"Leave me be, I beg of you," I heard her muffled voice say.

I pulled my hand away, remiss to obey, but unsure of what I could say. I spared a happened glance toward my finger.

A frown tugged at my lips. The merest hints of red stained the tips. I placed my hand back onto her wet sleeve, ignoring her half-protests of, *"Laura, please,"* and pulled it away, my breath hitching at my bloodied palm.

I remembered my vision of thirteen years past, of the ghastly specter who cried streaks of blood, the one who bore Carmilla's visage. "Carmilla," I said, harsher than I felt, "show me your face."

Beside me, Carmilla whimpered, and so I repeated my sudden command. "Show me your face."

She froze, utterly still.

"Carmilla—!"

I shrieked when Carmilla suddenly turned toward me, her face a mess of viciously vibrant streaks of blood, her eyes a void of black. Fangs protruded from her full lips as she bared her teeth, threatening to pierce the skin, and her nails had sharpened, hardened, gnarling into horrid claws.

I should have known, for my dream had warned me so.

We stared at the other, her face slowly twisting in fury, creating a macabre, gore-streaked glower.

Then, a knock at the door cut the tension between us. "Carmilla!?"

Madam Perrodon's voice held fear. I glanced at Carmilla, saw her eye the window, and I immediately, frantically, said, "'Tis only me, Madam!" Carmilla looked back to me, visibly startled despite her monstrous features. "Carmilla, silly thing, gave me quite a start and I screamed. All is well."

I looked back to Carmilla, still tense and ready to pounce—toward the window, I knew.

And I would never see her again if she did.

"Oh, heavens child—you will be the death of me. Do hurry up—your father wishes to leave for town soon."

"Of course, Madam," I replied, and I waited until her footsteps disappeared before I looked back to Carmilla. She had not moved, her body utterly frozen and prepared to run, and for a moment, I saw not a nightmarish creature, no, but a pitiful, frightened girl.

From the pocket of my skirt, I withdrew a small, lace handkerchief and held it up, approaching Carmilla in slow, easy motions. "Let me wipe your tears," I whispered.

I knew not what I faced, only that she bore the visage of the woman I loved. When I held my handkerchief to her face, the white cloth blossoming in billowing, brilliant red, more seeped from her eyes. She began to sob—from relief, from fear, I did not know, only that she clutched her arms, as though embracing herself. I hesitated to hold her, fearing bloodstains on my dress, so I placed my arm around her back as she cried.

I planted a kiss into her hair, kept blotting at her face though it did nothing to staunch her flow of tears. Carmilla's tears dripped onto the floor, but stone could be wiped clean. All would be well.

And when her sobs had dwindled into whimpers, though she still refused to face me, I said, "Tell me, truly, Carmilla—was it a dream, that night long ago?"

As she trembled, she shook her head.

My own shock had hardly settled, but my composure remained, as much for her as for me. "Will you look at me, please?"

She obeyed, those shined, black pits settling onto me. Her tears remained wet and vibrant on her face, but no more flowed. Though her fangs still protruded, I saw no menace; only teeth too large for her mouth, an abused animal prepared to fight.

I forced myself to smile, finding it easier than I expected. When I set the drenched handkerchief aside, I instead pulled the sheet from her messy bed. Blankets could be replaced, and I let the cloth soak up the drying tears upon her face. Her shock outmatched my own.

I spat upon the cloth, and when she did not flinch, I wiped the dried streaks from her face. In utter silence, for fear of startling her, I worked, and as the blood cleared color returned to her beautiful, enormous eyes. Her fangs retracted; her hands became soft.

I saw the face of the woman I loved, the girl who called me *'darling'* and kissed as though the world might end. "They are expecting us downstairs," I said, folding the blanket across my arm. I moved toward the dresser, stashing it for the moment. Upon our return, I would discard it into the lake. "Carmilla, come with us, but will you swear to tell me all once we are alone again?"

I watched her nod, unease still palpable in her stiff form. "I will tell you what I can."

My existential despair seemed a small thing for the moment. When I offered a hand, she accepted, as frail as I'd ever seen when she stood up. She nearly fell into my arms, my embrace all that kept her standing.

If she were a monster out to ruin me, would she not have done it long ago?

The Forest of Styria spread vast before us, but around the road the trees had long ago been cleared. A beautiful day, punctuated by brilliant sunlight and an appreciated breeze, and I breathed in the clean air, my fears feeling small. Though the carriage held walls and a roof, I kept the window open, let my hand and occasionally my hair whip about in the wind.

My father sat across me on the opposite bench of the carriage, a book in his hand that he leisurely skimmed. Carmilla lay across my lap, head cushioned by my thigh as she feigned sleep—the grip of her fist in the fabric of my dress told me she was wide awake.

The silence left time for contemplation, something I had done far too much of lately. This morning I had been in hysterics over our love affair, panic leading me to nearly drive her away, yet now . . .

All the world had changed. Everything I knew or thought I knew seemed shaky at best. God watched over us all, but now I shoved thoughts of saints and sins aside, for how did someone like Carmilla fit into this narrative? Churches taught of devils come to tempt mortals down to their fiery domain, yet though I knew the sin, my weakness, my wickedness, I could never see Carmilla as some creature of darkness. I ought to be afraid, to know I had given my body to some monstrosity from below. Hell spoke of demons, but Carmilla had spoken only of love.

My thoughts were a mystery too vast to solve. Instead, I rested my hand upon her back and felt her curl into the touch.

For hours, I heard only the faint crunching of dirt beneath the carriage wheels, but soon our destination came. From the window, I watched houses steadily appear by the roads, ever-increasing in scattered numbers. Noises from the town coaxed me to attention, and I smiled, overjoyed at the prospect of excitement and company even if the occasion were somber.

Yet, I flinched at the sight of the cathedral. The funeral would be held outdoors, as per Annette's father's request, but the old, brick church would shadow the affair. I hid my face within the carriage, the fear in my heart apparent once more.

When the carriage rolled to a stop, I felt Carmilla slowly rise. "Have we already arrived? Seems I slept the entire journey." She yawned to punctuate her words, and I questioned if it were real or false—I wondered if she even breathed at all.

"You must have needed it then, dear Carmilla," my father said, paternal affection in his gaze. The driver of our carriage opened the door, and when my father stepped out, he offered a hand to help the two of us. "Do tell us if your health begins to fail. We are here to honor the dead, but we cannot forget the living."

"My health is as unpredictable as the wind and rains," Carmilla replied, accepting his hand. "At times I have the stamina of merely a three-year-old child, and other times I have the capacity to skip and dance as the rest."

She smiled, and I wondered if any of her words were true now. I could not deny the frailty I had felt beneath her skin, how I had supported her through our numerous walks.

"I would only hate to find that your health had languished in our company," my father said as he helped me from the carriage. I immediately returned to Carmilla's side, surprised at my own protective instinct. "Do you expect to hear at all from your mother?"

"I do not know. I suppose I hope to, if only to know she is well."

I felt her hand slip into mine as she leaned her head against my shoulder. The affection made me shy, but so long as I showed nothing, there could be nothing amiss to see. There was no reason to think anything untoward; we were merely friends sharing sisterly affection.

God, it felt so wrong to even think. I had opened myself to her in ways too wicked and divine to speak of.

"Should you need to reach her," my father said, leading us to the collection of chairs beside the church, "simply tell me where to send the letter."

The service had already started, I was remiss to see. The sexton stood beside the open casket, speaking words I could only barely hear as we sat ourselves at the back. Carmilla took the seat beside me and wrapped her arm around mine. She had always been affectionate and flirtatious, but lately her actions had been fueled by a palpable undercurrent of desperation. I wondered at that, adding it to the ever-expanding list of mysteries writing the page of Carmilla in my life.

My stomach threatened to burst from a want to know all. Carmilla's ghastly transformation this morning, her admittance of being the player in my dream—all of it prickled in my mind, yet she herself had not changed.

As the service went on, I felt Carmilla slowly slide down, watched her cover her eyes from the sun. Even I, in my black silk and lace, felt the sun's weight; I feared what it would do to her.

"Carmilla," I whispered, "are you unwell?"

My father heard my words and glanced over to watch our interaction. Carmilla flinched from the sun as she gazed up at me. "I could do with some time in the shade. But I do not wish to—"

"Impose? Oh, Carmilla." Silently, I stood, then offered a hand to help her rise. "The dead will remain dead, but I do not wish for you to join them." I turned to my father, watched his concern on behalf of Carmilla. "We will be back soon."

He nodded his assent. I placed my hand on Carmilla's waist and led her away from the crowd. She whispered, "Your father grants you considerable freedom."

"As someone who revels in impropriety, I am amused you'd even notice." I teased, laughing at her amusement. "My father raised me alone in my apparent tower. To escort me everywhere would've been silly, so it has become habit for me to step away alone, even in public." The cathedral towered above us. "The church should be unlocked—"

"No." Carmilla's wide eyes were suddenly alert. She shook her head, frantic in her motions. "Not the church. The breeze will do me well, so long as we can find some shade."

"The shade it shall be," I replied, and I led her toward a collection of trees beside the great cathedral. Dew clung to the grass, so shaded it was, and when I helped her sit, she looked near collapsing. "Carmilla, are you sincerely unwell?" I asked, hating the implied accusation. But it had to be said. "Everything I know of you is suspect."

With her back to the tree, I saw her curl into herself. Her grand gestures of delight had ceased for now, replaced by palpable anxiety, and it wounded me to see. "I told you, my Laura, I have my vow—"

"I cannot pretend I did not see what happened this morning. I cannot go on not understanding. Why must you have this vow?"

"Laura, please," she begged, and I saw her fists clench in the grass, "you do not understand what you ask of me."

I frowned and sat beside her, placing my hand at her shoulder. "Who would care?"

"My momma." Her jaw began to tremble. I watched her fight her tears. "Please, Laura, for both of our sakes, ask me nothing."

"And what do we have to fear—"

"Everything!" she exclaimed, and I shied at her outburst. But she cringed, waving her hand at her eyes as though it might staunch her tears. "Laura, you will understand in time, I swear, but I cannot say much more—lest we lose it all."

I pulled a fresh handkerchief from my pocket and dabbed it at her eyes, noting the seeping red. "Tell me what you can," I whispered, allowing her to steal the cloth from me. "Please, Carmilla."

We were alone in this little bit of shade, no people in sight. I knew not who to thank for this blessing, but I was grateful, nonetheless. "As I said, I was the woman in your dream. And no, it was no dream," she said, as soft as the breeze lightly tussling her hair. "A moment of weakness, on my part. I could not stay away any longer."

The threat of her tears had dwindled. Still, she clutched the handkerchief. "I do not understand," I said, but she shook her head. "But then, when your carriage crashed near my home, was it fate or conspiracy?"

Carmilla remained silent a moment, and when she shut her eyes, she turned to stone, so still she sat. When she whispered, I leaned in to hear. "I can say nothing of my history with my momma, nor of the life I currently lead. But I can tell you of the life I lived before."

I came close to her, our shoulders pressed together. "My name is not Carmilla," she continued. "Though it is so desperately beautiful when I hear it from your tongue, my Laura. No, my given name was Mircalla, and I was born in the year 1680."

My breath left me all at once. "So, that portrait—"

"Is me, yes," she finished. Again, I saw fear in her dark, watery eyes, but behind it, peaceful reminiscence. "Countess Mircalla Karnstein, meant to inherit the very castle ruins your family keeps upon a hill. Back then, it was a splendid sight, built of gleaming stone. I was all but a princess, raised in grandeur and doted upon from birth." She met my eye now, losing that wistful glow. "The painting was my wedding portrait, and it certainly did capture my likeness."

Her story sparked questions with no answers she could give. I clung to every word. I would have been ashamed to admit it, but had I not witnessed the vile transformation of her body not hours before, I might have disbelieved her. But now, with everything I had ever learned suspect, I absorbed it like a young child.

"What I tell you," she continued, and I stole her hand when it began trembling. She paused, looked at my hand, and let hers fall limp. "What I tell you, I say not to invoke pity, but to convey the truth. You asked. This is what I may say." Her eyes fell shut. I watched as some distant pain twisted her features, nigh imperceptibly. Above, the birds sang, the sun remained bright, and at the base of the tree was tentative peace. "I was married to Baron Heinrich Vordenburg a week after the portrait was painted—for although the wedding was saturated in scandal, my family held wealth enough to sweep it beneath the rug."

She remained limp. I stayed silent, for although I was curious, I felt the bombardment of her memories, the pain she felt behind her eyelids. I could not help myself—I reached up to cup her cheek and kissed her hair, then pulled her into my arms.

"I told you of the masquerade—it was held by his family, and it was there I met Heinrich. Exhausted from festivities and intoxicated beyond what was lady-like, I bid the evening farewell and isolated myself in a library in the Vordenburg castle. I was followed by Heinrich, who proclaimed his drunken affection, and though I protested his advances, I was much too drunk to fight. I remember very little, but the night ended in pain . . . and in my pregnancy."

Carmilla fell into my embrace, letting the handkerchief fall to the ground as she clung to my body. I felt her breath—I suppose she did breathe—escape in a single, steadying sound. "I was so naïve; a romantic, thinking I might come to love him. The reputation of his temper preceded him, but his family was rich and I was beautiful—thus, we were wed to hide the scandal. But nothing, not even our unsavory, drunken beginning, could have prepared me for his cruelty. The memory of my wedding night is stained with tears, but it was merely the beginning of a journey through Hell. I gave him everything, but he stole even more."

I pressed Carmilla's face into my shoulder, her words cutting me down to my soul.

"However, I was beside myself with joy at the swelling in my stomach." Against the fabric of my dress, I did not feel her smile. "I feared my husband, but a child would be a spot of warmth amidst the cold. If I could not love Heinrich, perhaps I could love my baby. But pregnancy took a toll on my body, and I was largely resigned to bed." She curled tight, and I gripped her with all the strength I could muster, praying to remind her she was not alone. "At five months, he returned home after a failed night of gambling. He demanded my attention, the stench of bourbon on his breath, but I protested, for fear of harming the baby. My refusal sent him into a rage—"

I heard the hitch in her breath, and then she whispered, "I should not speak of it here, for fear of tears. But I lost the baby; that much is enough. It sent me spiraling into the depths of a depression I cannot describe in words. I saw my life as the cage it truly was, living in fear of a monster I could not fight. Like the life within my womb, all hope of happiness flickered out.

"It is among the most grievous sins," she continued, "to take a life, even if that life is your own. But I acquired a poison, as was much too easy to do in that time, and beneath the full moon's light in my window, consumed the entire draught—and died within minutes."

She pulled away from my arms, and I let her go, too shocked to speak. The truth of her story settled in my mind, and I saw her, then, as she was, the whispers of priests and the writings in horror books telling of legends too dark to speak, too wicked to be real.

Yet here she sat. I had seen her monstrous form for myself. If suicide did not lead directly to Hell, stories were told of a different path one's soul might take.

Carmilla met my eye, human in her gaze. "Forgive me," I said, and I saw her prepared to flinch, "but I dare not falsely accuse you of something so . . ." I trailed off, wondering how best to finish. Wicked? Unnatural? By God—was this a dream? ". . . impossible."

"I arose as a vampire," Carmilla whispered. Those impossible words fell from her tongue in gentle droves, so many truths of her strange and terrible habits having become clear. "The punishment for suicide in that era was worse than even now—today, you would be denied burial rights on holy ground, but then, your body was run through the streets and left to rot among the refuse. And so, the family kept it secret, claimed I died of sepsis from the miscarriage. I was placed within the mausoleum beneath my family's castle, but that very night, I walked out on my own accord."

I reached up to touch her cheek, finding it warm and flush with life. She watched every motion with unblinking eyes, tears threatening to well once more, for I held her future in my hands.

And I contemplated, in those tense moments of silence, what my heart made of this news, my worried heart that feared my abominable sins. For Carmilla was a woman, yes, one whom I loved and had made love to, but also a creature of darkness and depravity. I knew the tales of vampires; I knew what they consumed. They spat in the face of the Lord and his teachings, too wicked for Heaven yet refusing to be thrust down to Hell for their iniquities.

Something shifted in my resolve as I stared into her visage, the first step toward a life deviant from the one intended for me. Carmilla waited. I asked her simply, "Shall I call you Mircalla?"

She laughed. By God, she laughed, and I swore it was only to hold back tears. Relief flooded the gesture, and joy—boundless joy—though she visibly fought to not sob. "No, no, my darling. Mircalla died some two hundred years ago; let me live this new life with you."

I looked to the road and, finding it abandoned, kissed her on the mouth; reckless, yes, utterly stupid, but I could not resist the pull. Carmilla needed to know of my love, that my affection remained. I knew not my future with her, but I knew that singular, inalienable truth—that I had missed her all my life.

When I pulled away, she gasped and said, "Someday you shall know the rest, my love. But I thank you for listening."

"Thank you for trusting me."

70

"You did not reject me when you saw me as a monster." Still, I saw relief in Carmilla's breathless expression. "And for that, I would give you anything."

I reached up to cup her face, blushing when she turned into the gesture and kissed my palm. "So, what does it mean? You're a . . ." I dared not say the word too loud, instead lowering my voice to whisper. ". . . .vampire. Are all the stories true? By your own admission, you have passed two hundred years of age."

She shied, reached up to grip my wrist, then kept her hold tight as she lowered it down. "Much is true, and much is embellished. I mustn't enter a home uninvited, I cannot lie but can bend the truth with a bit of clever wordplay—hence my affection for anagrams of my name. The name 'Carmilla' is my favorite of them." Her smile faded as her attention fell to the shadowy cathedral. "I am cast out of Heaven's grace, and so symbols of divinity will harm me. And, yes—my ill health can be attributed to my state of being. I weaken in the sun; left to my own habits, I am entirely nocturnal."

She was so lively in the moonlight; at night, Carmilla reached her peak.

"There is more I shouldn't say, the reason I languish as I do, but I am sincere in my ill health. I've always appreciated your kindness in accommodating me."

"And what of . . ." Again, I hesitated, fearing to tread upon Carmilla's sensitivities, but even more so to speak and risk the great, looming cathedral hearing of it. "What of blood?" I whispered.

Immediately, Carmilla's grip tightened, in tandem with her chest caving forward. "We need not speak of something so vile, my darling Laura," she sputtered, and she refused to meet my eye, even as I looked to her. Instead, she kept her gaze fixed on the grass. "Only know that it is the cruel reality of my existence."

I heard singing come from afar. A somber tune; it seemed the funeral had ended. I hummed along with the familiar requiem, feeling the words rise in my throat, *"I need thee, oh I need thee—"*

But I stopped when Carmilla groaned and put her hands at her ears. "I beg of you, do not join with my torturers. Far too shrill a tune."

I stopped, unsure if I should take offense. But she kept her hands up, her face scrunching in pain as the distant song grew louder. "Cast out from divinity," I whispered, recalling her words. "I forget how much our lives are saturated in it."

She whimpered a pitiful, "Yes," as her fingers clutched her hair. In careful measures, I placed my hand upon her head and gently coaxed her down into my lap where my dress and hands could muffle her ears.

She seemed appeased, for I felt her fully relax.

The funeral procession had begun, the casket—now closed—carried toward the distant graveyard. We remained secluded behind the trees and the church, but as they passed us by I waved at my father, his searching gaze softening when he spotted us. He broke away from the revelry, frowning when he saw Carmilla's face all but hidden in my dress. "Is she all right?"

"A sudden headache," I replied, "but it will pass."

And it did—once the procession had made its way forward, the singing grew steadily distant. Carmilla lifted her head. "I am well enough," she said softly, her smile languid as she gazed from my father to me.

"I spoke to Annette's father a moment as the crowd gave its final respects," my father said, contemplation twisting his features as he watched the procession. "Apparently her sickness was quite sudden—at first nothing amiss, but then she began to speak of some beast in her nightmares. Her death came in only a week's time. She died of blood loss."

I felt myself frown. "How very strange."

I dared not look at Carmilla, for I feared, with this new knowledge of supernatural nightmares, that I might see a damning truth upon her features. A question for another time.

"Strange and tragic," I heard Carmilla agree. "Best we lock our windows at night; who can say what ungodly creatures may attempt to steal us?"

"I am much more concerned of a plague. The servant girl in our household claimed similar visions. Perhaps a call to the physician is in order—it might do you well anyway, Carmilla, given your ill health."

She shook her head, and I finally dared to gaze at her, admiring her commitment to her act. "You are too kind, but countless physicians have examined me. I live on, despite my trials." She laughed, and the sound dampened even my own fears—so lovely and musical a thing! "My momma always teased that trials were a gift from God, meant to mold us into his image. I suppose I will be his mirror before my life is through."

Utter blasphemy, yet I could not help but smile, even as her laughter increased.

As it was, even my skeptic father shifted uncomfortably. "A woman of odd humor, your mother," he said simply. "Are there any sights to see before we leave for home?"

Carmilla's disposition only continued to wilt. "Papa, we should leave for home, lest we lose Carmilla to exhaustion."

She smiled at me gratefully before setting her head into my lap.

"Are you afraid of me?" she asked

Against her lips, I whispered, "No."

That night, we moved as lovers would, our clandestine tryst as soft as a breeze of night. Carmilla fell into my arms, keeping my gaze as she gasped beneath me, succumbing to my touch. I loved it so, the power I wielded, the surge of pleasure from every whisper of my name enough for my own desire to nearly peak.

When she came undone, I held her softly to my heart, kissing her head as she whispered, "My darling, the joy I feel with you ..." I felt her shudder against me and knew she must be fighting tears.

I soothed her hair with fine strokes of my hand. "May I ask something?"

"You may," she whispered. My breasts pressed against either side of her face, the intimacy of it still so new. "And I will answer, if I am able."

"I do not yet know how to accept . . . or *explain* . . ." I trailed off, realizing I meandered around my intended query. "How did you come to realize you loved women?" My own held breath released. "Much less accept it?"

She shifted in my arms, and I felt her gaze even before I looked down to match it. "Do you still fear the sin?"

Yes, and yet it seemed a muted thing compared to the realization of Carmilla's true character. But I spoke the truth when I said, "I do."

"I do not know if I believe in God," Carmilla said. "Because it means he created a creature like me, only to condemn me to Hell from the start."

I knew not if she referred to being a vampire or her habit of kissing women. Yet the words were dangerous to think, much less say, and so I stared at her, aghast.

But she stroked her hand across my face, sweeping aside errant strands of hair. "I do not fear the sin. I have pursued my joy for nearly two hundred years and have not been struck down yet." Carmilla placed a gentle kiss upon my chin, then shifted up, keeping our faces level to the other. "Like you, I was raised largely isolated upon a hill, lonesome more often than not. I knew not that I favored women, only that I had given little regard to the men who pursued me. When I married Heinrich, I sincerely thought I might come to love him once I knew him. It was not until I rose after my death that I ever felt free to see and understand the world, and it was because of momma that I—"

Carmilla cut herself off. "I have said too much," she whispered.

"So, you have loved other women?" The thought caused ice to seep into my veins, but I forced my composure to keep steady. Never had I thought I might be one prone to jealousy, but the thought of Carmilla touching another woman filled me with unparalleled fury.

Carmilla nodded. "But all for pleasure; not for love. I meant as I said—that I had been in love with no one." Her lips pressed against mine, her kiss reassuring and tender all at once. When she pulled away, she smiled as gently as the nighttime breeze. "Except now. For I sincerely and truly love you."

She had said as much before, yet every time it caused my heart to soar. "I love you," I whispered, and I pressed our lips together once again. Her hands caressed my naked body, lingering at the curves of my waist, my breasts. When she kissed my chest, I felt the sting of her teeth, her proclivity to leave marks something dangerous and endearing all at once.

I still knew not what future could be ours. But her hands touched every part of me, my soul fully open to her presence, and I wondered if heaven was not a place, no, but a state of being, the time where one might exist with God or whatever deity they claimed.

Carmilla did not believe in God, but she believed in me.

Carmilla's visitations pushed later and later into the night. I awoke one morning well past my usual hour, only to stumble upon my father in the parlor as I made my way to breakfast.

"Good morning, papa," I mumbled, dressed in my chemise and robe. I planned to say my 'hellos' and then return to bed, exhausted from a night I dared not speak of.

Guilt filled me at the thought. I knew not what to think of anything anymore. But before I could contemplate it further, my father said, "Good morning, my Laura." He beckoned me forward, a frown on his face. "You look unwell."

"I hardly slept," I said truthfully. "Tossed and turned for most of the night."

"Laura, there was another death among the servants last night—a girl your same age."

My heart sank at the news.

"The body has been sent to the physician for inspection." Genuine worry shone in his countenance, and my father was not one to entertain fruitless feelings of anxiety. "Some of the servants have deemed it supernatural. I fear it may be a plague. Two girls have died, and not unlike how Annette passed away, or so says her father. Some feverish insanity accompanies it—all of them claimed to have dreams of monstrous visitors in the night—" He stopped quite suddenly, his frown growing deep. "You say you could not sleep? Did you dream?"

I shook my head, but a glower settled onto my features. Once, I would have scoffed, like my father, at any notion of supernatural activity. A certain vampiric woman had cured me of that particular sort of skepticism.

"If you would excuse me, I am much more tired than I thought—"

"Laura, will you spare a moment first? We need to talk."

He gestured to the seat beside him; I obeyed and settled in. "Papa?"

"The cook asked me last night when your wedding to the general would be held."

My stomach quite suddenly grew hollow.

"I dissuaded her of the rumor, but I asked where she had heard it—apparently, all the servants are talking about it. Who did you tell?"

The reminder of my future paled to the cold numbing my limbs. "I confided in Carmilla. Papa, I am so sorry."

"What did you tell her?"

"The truth," I implored, shame coloring my cheeks. "That I hadn't decided but I would at least give it thought. She teased me of it later, in the ballroom—someone must have overheard."

He sighed, adding to my shame. His disappointment in me was so rare. "Let us pray my staff says nothing to General Spielsdorf when he visits. He would be terribly embarrassed—and insulted, if you were to reject him after all this scandal."

76

With my lips pursed, I swallowed my shame, his implications as clear as the heat on my cheeks. "May I be excused?" I whispered, the very air growing stifling by the second.

He agreed, and I left. I did not go to my bedroom but to Carmilla's, where I rapped on the door with my knuckles.

I heard nothing. When I knocked again and nothing happened, I swallowed my fear and prayed it were merely some vampiric quirk yet to be explained.

Instead of panicking, I stole a page from my journal and wrote the words *find me*. When I had slipped the page beneath her door, I returned to my bedroom.

Too anxious to sleep, I sat in my bed and resorted to writing. My evening ritual had once been to write of my day, even if my day consisted of the same activities as the previous, but in as illustrious terms as I could evoke. An exercise—one to improve my writing and to cast a bit of enjoyment onto my quiet life.

Ironic, then, that since Carmilla's coming, since excitement had entered my lonely existence, I had neglected my nightly habit, at first afraid of my own burgeoning feelings and now to give priority to her visits.

My pen trembled as I wrote her name, afraid to implicate myself, but the words flowed like an evocative river, the night we'd first kissed pulsing in my mind. Perhaps it was to make sense of it, to siphon through my knowledge and find a creature of darkness, yet all I wrote of was light.

Near noon, a light knock pulled me from my literary musing. The knob turned, and thus entered Carmilla, smiling as though all was well, as though she weren't responsible for the deaths of our servant girls, nor of my friend from town.

That smile remained infectious. I returned it and beckoned for her to come.

Carmilla shut the door and joined me in bed, our lips touching before she muttered, "Good morning," against them.

When she deepened the kiss and slipped her tongue into my mouth, I dropped my book and pen, splattering ink across the sheets as I clutched her face between my hands. I heard her moan against me, felt her wandering hands upon my nightgown, shy and yet bold in her way. Spurred by her touch, I coaxed her down, thoughtless as I straddled her waist and kissed her sweet neck.

Consumed in her scent, I forgot the whole world.

A knock, and then the doorknob twisted. I sat up, nearly toppling over as Mademoiselle De Lafontaine peeked her head in. Her hair, perfectly coiffed, held strands of grey, but her face was hardly so put together. "Mademoiselle?" I said, forcing my breathing to steady. I feared the blush upon my cheeks, but not so much as I feared her thoughts.

"Are you coming for your lesson?" she asked, and I prayed my face hid my relief.

Carmilla sat up, serene in her graceful movements. "'Tis my fault, mademoiselle. Laura was kind enough to finally reveal her secret writings to me." She glanced at my book, forgotten on the sheets. "I distracted her."

"The day is half done—find me in the study once you're dressed."

She shut the door. I turned to Carmilla and said, "We cannot let ourselves be carried away."

"Tragically, I must agree." Carmilla sat up. She gently stole the book from the bed, stroking the leather with her lithe fingers before adding, "Will you show me? For fear of making a liar out of me to your governess."

She winked, but her request was sincere. Shy, I took the book and opened it to my last bit of writing. "I had to release the words," I whispered, nervous as I gave it back. "They'll be burned once you read them, lest someone else stumble upon them."

Carmilla's gaze softened as her large eyes skimmed the written words. Tears welled in her eyes, but I watched her swallow them back. "Such lovely turns of phrase you have," she said, smiling as she fought her welling emotion. *"With her skin awash in moonlight, she glowed like the holy angels above..."* she recited, my own words beautifully trailing off her tongue. "And here I am, a creature cast out even from Hell. So beautiful, the way you see me. I do not deserve you."

She masked her poignant words behind a teasing smile. I stole her hand, my response welling from the depths of my very soul. "I love you."

Carmilla brought my hand to her lips and kissed it, lighter than summer rain. "Then let the fire that burns these pages seal our future in flame."

I trembled to think of the future but swallowed my fear. Now was not the time, not with Carmilla's beautiful face all but aglow. "We should go," I said, remiss at my words. "Mademoiselle De Lafontaine is furious as it is."

Carmilla's grin bespoke mischief. "Dressing a woman can be as intimate an affair as undressing one, you know. Let me help you, my darling."

I thrust aside thoughts of my inevitable engagement, instead content to bask in Carmilla's teasing touch. To savor every moment together would be enough. It would have to be enough.

Chapter Three

All of these feelings, so wondrous and new. Guilt was for the outside world; it held no place in my bed.

That night, my touch lingered, trailing her pleasure until the moon had set and she whimpered beneath me, begging for release. She shuddered and sobbed upon climax, staining the pillowcase in streaks of brilliant red.

A creature of darkness in my bed, a recreation of that vision, some thirteen years ago . . . but this time, I held her to my breast, uncaring of the blood staining my flesh. I'd burn the pillowcase in the fireplace or bury it in the haunted woods of Styria—for now, Carmilla needed me. All the world was silent.

The sky held hints of daylight—it would be less than an hour more. "I may request we simply sleep tomorrow night," I whispered, unable to help my smile when she turned her gaze upon me. "Lest my father think me ill. He already worries about my exhaustion."

"Whatever you need, my darling, darling." Carmilla placed a kiss upon my cheek, her body trembling—from tears or pleasure, I did not know. "We have time yet."

The warmth brimming from my heart froze at those weighted words. She knew, then. She knew the impending heartbreak between us. Rather than confront it, I stole her mouth with mine, my own burning need for her touch simmering, longing to boil.

She worshipped my body like the God she did not believe in, the sharp sting of her bites shocking pleasure through my veins. Blood stained my body; her presence stained my soul. Unbidden, I moaned, and when she kissed between my legs, I released a sharp cry—one I immediately bit back.

Footsteps sounded through the hall.

"Carmilla," I whispered, frantic.

She looked up at me, licking her lips, when the door handle twisted. "Trust me—"

"Laura—!?" Madam Perrodon shrieked, as did I. Dim light from the window revealed what her candle could not, and before I could blink Carmilla became a shadowed, cat-like beast. Refractive eyes, the color of her own when they bled precious blood, shone, along with fangs glinting in the light. "Monster!" the madam cried, but before she could speak again, the beast dove off my bed and to the window. Glass shattered as she disappeared into the night.

I heard commotion arise from the halls. Madam Perrodon ran to my side, hysterical as she shrieked. I realized my nakedness lay exposed. Gasping, I grabbed the sheets, but Perrodon wept. "Laura, what has happened? By God—you're dying!"

I began sobbing. From my misted vision, I saw Mademoiselle De Lafontaine rush in, as well as a number of servants. Perrodon remained distraught as she relayed what she had seen, citing the ruined window and bloodied sheets as evidence. "I saw it—a beast loomed over our dear Laura."

My father ran in, ghostly white saturating his features. "Call the physician!" he cried, anger marring his panic. "My daughter is dying! *Go!*"

A few servants scattered. I clutched the sheet to my naked body as I cried. "Not dying," I managed to spit through my alarm. "I-I'm not hurt."

De Lafontaine had said nothing, merely inspected my flesh for wounds. Her shaking hands on my skin were all that spoke of her fear. The bed shifted; my father joined us, his gaze averted from my exposed skin. "What happened?"

Perrodon sputtered her tale, of how she'd heard my cry and seen a beast leering before me.

Daylight burst from the window. My heart raced, and all I could do was silently berate my own foolishness.

"Carmilla," Mademoiselle De Lafontaine suddenly gasped. "Where is Carmilla? Someone check on the poor girl!"

The remaining servants ran. My father said, "Laura, what do you know?" He looked near weeping as well—I saw the streaks of blood reflected in his glossy eyes.

"I-I—" My sobs overwhelmed me, fear and shock cutting off my ability to speak. "I do not know. I awoke at the madam's entrance." My jaw shook furiously—my words were hardly intelligible, I was certain.

"It is as the servants said," my father muttered, "that the dead dreamt of a beast in the night."

"Laura, please tell us everything you remember," De Lafontaine said; Madam Perrodon still struggled to breathe.

"I-I do not know, I swear. Perhaps I dreamt of—"

"What did you dream?" my father interrupted, his stare suddenly sharp upon the blemish below my collarbone.

I shied at the scrutiny, attempting to hide the mark with my hair, but he came forward and brushed it aside. "It is very important that you relay everything, my Laura. Your life may depend on it."

Of course I lied, though it bespoke well enough of the truth in my panic. I stumbled through the tale of a passionate dream, demure at the details, but clear in the implication of intimate touching—lest there be evidence to implicate me in any sin. God would not judge what we did in a dream, and so neither would they. "Father, I do not understand—"

A servant burst in, cutting off my speech. "Pardon the intrusion, monsieur. But Mademoiselle Carmilla is missing!"

By God, no.

My fear showed, it seemed, for Perrodon held me to her breast, shushing my flowing tears. De Lafontaine spat, "For heaven's sake, gentlemen—clear the room so the girl may put on some clothing!"

With a curt sigh, my father nodded. "We shall organize a search party.

They left. The door shut, leaving me with only my governesses. "Laura," De LaFontaine said, clutching my hand, "we shall help you wash. The doctor will come; you shall not die this day."

I managed a nod, trembling as Perrodon wrapped me tight in a sheet.

They drew a bath, and only De Lafontaine managed to keep her wits about her—Perrodon wept at every streak of blood, and so did I, afraid for my heart, now missing from her bed. I remembered her panic when I first saw her monstrous form—she looked to the window, resolved to never return if I rejected her. I feared she would never be found.

They washed the blood from my hair and body, the only sigh of barrage my swollen face and the tender mark upon my breast.

The morning progressed, and I was doted upon. Dressed up in my finest nightgown, a plate of cookies and a cup of tea had been brought. Despite all the words of reassurance, I thought only of Carmilla—worried as to where she might've run. While bathing, my bed had been stripped and remade—fresh sheets awaited me. "The physician will be here any moment, I am sure," Perrodon said. Those were her first calm words of the day, though she had not left my side.

Her words proved prophetic; footsteps from beyond stole my attention. A knock, and Doctor Spielsburg and my father entered—in his arms, he held Carmilla, who lightly stirred. "She was in the grove of trees," he said, "fast asleep. Carmilla requested she be brought to you, once she heard there was a scare."

I could not help the fresh tears brimming in my eyes. I beckoned him forward, and he carefully placed the nightgown-clad young woman onto my bed. "It seems I slept-walked in the night," she whispered, her eyes as alert as I had ever seen. She wrapped her arms around my waist, protective as her hands gripped my chemise. "Tell me what has happened."

"Our Laura has been through a nightmare," Perrodon replied. I kept silent, however, my hands tangled in Carmilla's hair and gown. They could not implicate her. There was no proof.

I prayed my hope was true.

The doctor placed his bag at the foot of my bed. "They say you saw a beast."

Perrodon cried, "She was covered in blood!" She burst into tears yet again, gasping for breath, her face pale from shock.

"But held no injury," De Lafontaine added, casting her stern gaze onto Perrodon.

Doctor Spielsburg withdrew a stethoscope from his bag, but his gaze narrowed—I realize he looked at the mark by my breast, barely peeking above my chemise. "I-I told my father and my governesses—" My words stopped when I felt Carmilla's grip tighten at my waist. "I-I told them that I dreamt of something . . ." I cringed at the words on my tongue, feeling ashamed to say the truth. ". . . something intimate." Carmilla's touch lingered, as told by the touch on my nightgown. "I awoke when I heard Madam Perrodon's scream. And it is as she said—some beast was atop me."

Carmilla sat up when the doctor inspected my neck, her stare bright but her movements dreamy and slow. "Seems you have had quite the scare, my darling." She placed a hand on my neck and slid it up to cup my cheek.

The doctor placed his hand on my forehead. "You are terribly pale. But you say none of the blood was yours?"

I shook my head. My father tugged on the sleeve of his shirt, his lips thinned and nearly white. "I have sent my servants on a hunt for the beast," he said. "Terror aside, the blood might've been the remains of its last meal."

The doctor merely frowned, again staring at the peeking mark along the collar of my nightgown. "How long have you had that?"

"I cannot say—"

Perrodon interrupted, nearly gasping the words, "It has been a week at least, doctor. I saw it first when I helped her dress for Mademoiselle Annette's funeral."

So she had.

"With respect," De Lafontaine said, her frown growing severe, "you will only cause Laura to scare more with this behavior." She escorted Perrodon out, leaving Carmilla and I with my father and the doctor.

"Will you allow your father to pull down your collar? It will have no bearing on your modesty; only enough so I may inspect it further."

"Oh, let a lady do it," Carmilla said, sitting herself up. Her smile held nothing but sincerity, yet I sensed mischief in her tone. "Then there is no question upon her honor."

The doctor agreed, and Carmilla's soft fingers pulled at the nightgown, revealing the slight shadow of my cleavage. The deepening, sickly purple and yellow stood in stark contrast to my pale skin. The physician stared and muttered, "Do you recall when this occurred?"

Fighting my blush, I swallowed and said, "I do not know. I must have bumped it without realizing."

It remained a small spot, no larger than my thumbprint. Doctor Spielsburg stared, his smile vanishing entirely. I looked up and saw my father glowering, though his seemed saturated in confusion instead of worry. "Why are we concerned for a bruise when a wild animal is loose upon my grounds?"

"I fear it is no wild animal, monsieur." He turned to Carmilla. "And you? Any dreams? Any strange bruising?"

"No," she said, utterly serene. I realized her hand had settled instead to my waist, protective in her embrace.

Doctor Spielsburg looked to my father. "Let us confer alone, a moment."

"Why? What is going on?" I asked, as the two gentlemen left.

"Nothing to worry yourself over," the doctor replied. "I would not want you to hurt yourself from stress."

The implication of my weakness pulled a frown to my face, but he and my father left. Carmilla immediately kissed my cheek. "Silly men, worrying over a bit of sensuous bruising."

"Carmilla, this is not a joking matter. You've put my entire household in a panic. If my father does not send me away to France, he shall at least post servants in my bedroom."

But my companion merely grinned and continued kissing my cheek. "Darling, darling—if nothing else, I ask for your trust."

"And I ask for your discretion," I said, and as she gazed back at me, nothing but sincere affection in her eyes, the reality of our love affair, and the inevitable end and heartbreak, once again welled up in my stomach.

I could not imagine a life without her, yet our future remained so uncertain—for her mother would return, my hand would be given to the general, and from there—

"Laura?" Her hand brushed against the darkened circles of my eyes, wiping tears I had not known I'd shed.

"Later," I whispered, drying my eyes on my sleeve.

The doorknob twisted. My father entered alone, thoughtful as I frowned. "Doctor Spielsburg has gone to the servants' homes."

"Papa, what has happened? What did he say?"

"Nothing to worry about. You will be fine, but he insists you not be left alone."

"I would be thrilled to keep your daughter company," Carmilla said as she leaned her head against my shoulder.

My father smiled, age doing nothing to mar the glimmer in his eye. "We are blessed to have you, Carmilla. As happy as we shall be of her safe return, it will be a mournful day when your mother comes to steal you from us."

He saw himself out, Carmilla's expression remaining pleasant until the door shut. "Laura, tell me what plagues you," she said, reaching up to stroke my cheek.

Fatigue pulled at my eyelids, the scare finally settling, but I knew I would not sleep. "Let us get dressed," I replied, turning into the touch of her hand. "I would rather speak outside, lest we be overheard."

We held hands on the grassy lawn outside my father's house. A blatant display of affection, scandalous for couples, especially those unwed; yet for two women, I suppose it meant nothing—nothing more than sisterly affection.

I wondered if, in another life, we could have remained as such, with only friendly devotion binding us instead of passion and longing. I loved her—oh, I loved her—and still it scared me so, more than even the reveal of her supernatural character.

Odd, to think I could accept her as a vampire more easily than my peculiar fondness for her. A wiser person than myself would call it a manifestation of self-loathing, but I merely wanted to weep.

In the copse of trees, she suddenly stumbled—and, startled, I yelped as she fell to the ground. "Carmilla!" I cried, kneeling beside her.

She looked up and smiled, sorrow in the gesture. "I apologize. I feel particularly weak today—"

"Do not apologize. Are you hurt?" Despite my panic, the statement posed a query. "Are you capable of being hurt?"

Carmilla accepted my hand as I helped her to stand. "I am not nearly so fragile as you. Do not fret, my darling. It would take more than a fall to end me."

She leaned on me as we walked through the trees. "What was that creature?" I whispered, recalling the cat-like beast in my bed.

"Another manifestation of my monstrosity. I thought, if we were to be caught, to give them a real monster to fear, instead of the ardor of two women. Seems it worked."

Her apparent indifference infuriated me, but I daren't say so—shortsighted as her plan was, as idiotic as we had behaved, it had saved our secret.

For now. Until the next time we gave into our passion like the tragic fools we were.

We came upon the singing brook, shaded by trees and my own quiet anguish. Carmilla placed a tender kiss on my cheek. "Your silence is so incredibly loud. Please, say something."

Speckles of sunlight filtered through the grove. I gripped her tight as I spoke my dangerous words. "I know I must respect your vow. You cannot speak until your mother's return, but what then? Will you leave me?"

Carmilla said nothing, only stared as I led her through the shade.

"My life is so rapidly changing, Carmilla," I continued. "I told you I loved you, and I-I—" I stopped, swallowing back a sudden rise of tears. The brook whispered beside us; the crisp air bit at my skin, yet all the world dulled to her radiant face. "I am so scared, because of how desperately I mean it. I love you, Carmilla. What future do we have? Your mother will come, and perhaps you will visit—only to find me married to the general, locked away forever in my tower of security and comfort. I shall praise God with my husband, pray that my soul is not damned for my affection for you, all while longing for a future that can never be. Carmilla, I *know* you killed the servant girls. I shall not ask; I *know*. You killed Annette. You kill to stay alive; you hate it, but it must be done. You give in to your passions with the fearlessness of one already damned, but Carmilla, my love, my *heart . . .*" Sobbing now, I managed a gasping breath, my thoughts boiling over. "Carmilla, I am afraid."

Carmilla reached up, brushed the stray locks of my blonde hair away from my face, and whispered, "Come with me."

My breath hitched. The words settled into my senses; impossible, yes, damning in every way.

"Come with me," she repeated, with all the ardor of our nightly passions. "Come with me, even unto death, my darling, darling—" Her lips stole mine. We kissed in the daylight, in full view of my home, but instead of running, I clung to her. Carmilla's fragile form pressed against mine, held by my own limited strength.

Against my lips, she whispered, *"Laura, how I love you."*

By God, I loved her too.

I stole her away, deeper into the grove of trees, secluded in the shade and among the throng of nature. She succumbed as I touched beneath her dress, my tumultuous emotions softer than the whispered moans she gifted me. In the light of day, I saw each emotion cross her face, every smile and sob.

I did not dream. I longed for nothing more than to see her in the light.

For us to be able to stand in the light.

And when she shuddered and praised my name, I fell into her arms, cushioned by grass, shaded by trees. I kissed her perfect, dainty lips, then hid my face within her hair.

In my own head, I heard the repetition of her temptation: *"Come with me."*

What would it mean, to follow her to Hell?

"All that I have ever known is suspect," I whispered, even as her embrace grew tight.

In the distance, I heard conversation. I looked up, pulled from Carmilla's embrace, then heard a familiar voice cry, "Laura?"

My father approached. "Papa, we are here!" I yelled, and once I stood, I offered a hand to Carmilla. With our fingers intertwined, I looked into the distance and, indeed, saw my father but with him . . .

"General Spielsdorf," I whispered, recognizing the man. His hair greyed, though not so much as my father's, but instead of kindness in his disposition, I saw anguish; I saw *rage*.

". . . you come not to claim any titles or estates?" I heard my father say.

"Upon the conclusion of my quest, we may discuss a proposal, but I stopped by on my path to see Baron Vordenburg—"

Spielsdorf stopped, staring not at me but at Carmilla, shock twisting instantaneously to fury. "Fiend!"

He withdrew a gun.

Small hands shoved me to the ground. I heard a great *boom*. My father yelled, I sobbed, and when I regained myself, I saw not the Carmilla I knew, but the monster of my childhood nightmare who cried red, vicious tears. Here she held no weakness; here her claws wracked across the general's face, casting searing lines upon his cheeks.

Another *boom* and this time I heard Carmilla scream. From her shoulder blossomed a bud of silver, petals of red.

In the second before he might have shot again, I surged forward. No thought to my actions; I tackled the man with all my strength.

Due to surprise or adrenaline, I succeeded. "Carmilla, run!" I cried, and when I looked back, she had vanished.

My father pulled me up, his face sheet white. "Laura, what—"

"That is the very monster I told you of!" Spielsdorf cried, the welts at his face seeping blood. Breathing heavy, he looked to me, his crazed eyes settling into sorrow. "She is the girl who slew my Bertha."

I would have collapsed, had my father not been holding me. "What are you talking about?" I asked.

"That is Millarca," the general said, looking back to my father. "I swear to you, upon my life—and her monstrous face confirms it."

"I cannot deny it," my father whispered. "Laura—"

"Tell me," I pled, my face surely swollen from tears. "Who is Millarca? What is happening?"

Spielsdorf pulled a handkerchief from his pocket and held it to his wounded face, blood immediately staining the cloth. "Your daughter is in shock. We should take her inside."

But my father, when I looked at him, looked to be the one in shock. "The physician said it was some supernatural cause. The beast in your bed . . ." He stared at me, his jaw slack.

With a final burst of strength, I escaped his grasp and stumbled back, regaining my footing as a clung to a tree. I stared at General Spielsdorf, blood coursing through my veins, pounding in my eardrums. "Tell me."

"We met Millarca and her mother at Baron Vordenburg's ball, not five months ago." Spielsdorf removed the cloth from his face, cringing at the seeping blood. "Her mother implored me to let her daughter stay with us."

Something cold and piercing clutched my heart.

"Bertha and Millarca became fond friends, until she began to fall ill. By the time the doctor came, it was nearly too late. He instructed me to never leave her alone, that some evil beast had come to claim her."

My father had turned stark white. My hands trembled against the bark of the tree.

"And so I hid in Bertha's bedroom one night and witnessed the wicked act myself—that of Millarca biting her upon her breast."

Absently, I touched the tender mark upon my own.

"I rushed out with a sword. Millarca fled. Bertha lay dead in her bed. And I have sought to hunt the beast ever since."

My hand pressed against the bark of the tree, the imprint threatening to slice through my skin. Carmilla had said so herself—that I would follow her unto death.

But I shook my head. "No, no..." Fresh sobs wracked my body. I managed to stammer, *"Carmilla loved me,"* before I collapsed to the ground, grass cushioning my fall.

Through the static of my soul-wrenching cries, I felt my father's embrace. I felt the general's stare. Not minutes ago, I kissed her, moved within her, stole her for me, and knew that I, in turn, belonged to her.

Was this her game? I recalled her face. I heard the ardor in her words as she pled with me to *come with her.*

I had to find her. I had to know the truth.

"The doctor is still here. Laura, you must see him."

I allowed him to help me stand, my sobs muted, tears flowing fast. In a daze, I let him lead me to our home.

She would find me. But if not—

I suddenly recalled her words, her reminiscence of her home in Castle Karnstein, of the mausoleum beneath the ruins. Her tomb lay there, in the haunted woods—and so there she must return.

The doctor treated me for shock, forced me to drink water until I swore my stomach would burst, then prescribed me sleep. *"Laura will live, so long as the creature does not return."*

I wore a dress but no corset—Madam Perrodon insisted I would faint. Once the men had left, I stared out the window, plotting my hike to Castle Karnstein. The path would take hours on foot. It was treacherous enough in the day—at night, I did not know what horrors I might meet.

But truthfully, I sought the greatest horror of them all. Despite my denial, I courted death; I made love to death.

But had Carmilla done as much with all her victims? By God, I had to know.

I looked to Madam Perrodon, assigned to my bedside, who had hardly breathed in all her doting on me. She seemed to have recovered; pale, but not deathly so. "I still cannot believe it," she whispered, having followed my gaze to the window. "That Carmilla, the sweet thing, would be the greatest evil of all."

"Impossible for anyone to believe," I replied. I moved to my nightstand, and from the drawer withdrew the portrait of Countess Mircalla, recalling the damning tale behind it. Though the painting had faded with age, I saw her features clearly, done up in an antiquated style. I wondered of her life and death; I knew so little of her, aside from the pain hiding behind her pleasantries.

Beneath it lay my journal, the damning pages torn away and burned, forgotten, as would her impact in my life be should I not find her now.

"Madam, I need to relieve myself. You know the doctor made me drink my weight in water." I attempted to laugh, but Perrodon's jaw trembled as she met my eye.

"If you do not return within ten minutes, I will alert your father."

Her narrowed eyes spoke all—she knew my intentions.

But I smiled. "Of course."

Ten minutes to escape the window's gaze.

As silent as I could, I ran to the stairs, grateful the steps were carpeted. Within my father's office, I overheard Spielsdorf raging that, *"The fiend will not see another sunrise."*

I crept as softly as my heels would allow—the entry hall was tiled in stone. I glanced behind and saw the backs of a few men, some I did not know. I heard my father's voice: *"Baron Vordenburg, you say you've slain vampires before?"*

I knew the name—the baron lived at the other end of Forest of Styria; he had hosted the fateful ball where Bertha had met the so-called 'Millarca.' *"Too many times, and most of them stemmed from the monster who infiltrated your house,"* replied one with a rich manner of dress—I saw as much even staring at the back of his coat. *"For nearly two hundred years, my family has hunted the countess."*

And such was the name of Carmilla's monster of a husband—*Vordenburg*.

Another mystery to ask her, should I succeed in my impossible quest. I touched the doorknob. *"Laura?"* came a whispered voice.

I clenched my fist, fighting a gasp. Mademoiselle De Lafontaine stared from the dining room doorframe. The severity of her gaze spoke that she knew all. *"Please, no,"* I mouthed, desperately shaking my head.

She looked to my father's office. My heart ceased beating.

Silent steps came toward me. She kept her stare at his office all the while. I daren't move, and when she grabbed my arm, I nearly wept. *"They will hear you leave,"* she breathed, inaudible, and yet I understood. She tugged me along, both of us utterly silent. Down the hall, past statues and chandeliers, and to a servant's exit by the garden.

"Now go," she whispered, unlocking it with her keys. Sunlight burst through the door.

I stepped through, blinded by the influx of light. "I don't understand—"

In a gesture foreign to us both, Mademoiselle De Lafontaine pulled me close and hugged me tight. Skin and bones, this aging woman, yet I felt safety in her embrace. "A lifetime ago, I loved a girl in an acrobatics troupe who begged me to join her. I rejected her and have regretted it every day since. Find Carmilla."

Too shocked to respond, when she pulled away, I managed to nod, giving a final squeeze to her hands and darting away.

I hiked up my skirts and ran across the lawn, sunlight beaming though it promised to soon fade. I knew these grounds like the lines of my palm, having studied them just as often, knew the babbling brook beyond, even knew to leap before I traversed the bridge, recalling the loose bits of stone and gravel.

It was the forest that would swallow me whole.

My breath languished; my blood burned, but still I ran, even as the scene grew harsh and grey. Faint signs of daylight filtered through the trees, yet it promised a terrifying nightfall. The countryside whispered that the woods were haunted, that enchantments existed to steal away unwitting travelers. I was not raised on fairy tales, no—I had no fear of fae who might steal me away into the fog. Instead, my father warned me to never come alone for fear of starving beasts and disappearing forever in the endless mist.

Finally, I stopped, nearly collapsing from exhaustion. Birds sang high above, and I prayed the rustling of bushes and shrubbery meant rodents and nothing more. I knew not my destination, but I knew how to find it—seek a slope and follow it up. Castle Karnstein sat alone on a hill.

I walked until sunset.

Mist settled across the forest floor, casting eerie visions across the trees. Night creatures sang at my presence, ominous sounds to ward away any so foolish as to traverse the woods of Styria in the dark. The moist smell sent shocks of cold into my lungs, the condensation collecting in droplets upon my dirty skirt and bodice. Soon, I could barely see my own feet.

Then, I heard them. Howling in the night. My steps slowed, but still I heard rustling leaves.

Frozen, I stared into the mist, praying I imagined the glowing of a hundred eyes circling me in the darkness. Pine needles crunched as I stepped forward. I approached an incline—by God's grace, the hill upon where Castle Karnstein sat stood nigh.

My thighs burned, my leisurely walks along my father's estate hardly proper preparation for hiking uphill. My destination neared, though, the mere thought spurring me forward. Whether it led to heartbreak or hope, the promise of answers awaited.

But a vicious snarling signified my end.

The mist parted for a tower of stone, but below appeared an enormous wolf, one with golden eyes and scraggly fur. The first of many—the pack emerged from the fog, all of them half-starved. Wolves were shy creatures—I knew this from my skeptic father and his books. But starving creatures would threaten a human.

Eat them, even.

Though fear threatened to consume me, I bore my teeth as father's books had taught, snarling as I stepped forward, standing tall. The alpha wolf growled, but to my utter amazement, it shrunk at my approach.

"Go!" I cried, hoping noise might scare it off. "All of you! Go!"

Another step forward, and the wolf moved back. For a fleeting moment, I thought I might live.

From the mist, a monster charged. I screamed, falling back as it landed beside me. Feline in its form, it bore claws and nails larger than the wolf's head, teeth that consumed its mouth. It reared upon its hind legs, taller than myself, and roared.

The wolves scattered, gone into the mist in seconds.

Even as I turned to face the creature, I saw it shrink, its claws and teeth vanishing. All semblance of her beastly form disappeared, leaving only Carmilla in a day dress. "Welcome to my home," she whispered, no grandeur in the phrase.

As I studied the dilapidated structure, she took my hand in hers. Through the mist appeared the image of a castle, or the ruins thereof. Entire walls were stripped away, collapsed from time and disuse.

She led me not to the castle, but toward the collapsed entrance of what seemed to be an underground cave. From her pocket, she pulled a small box, lit a match, and illuminated the ancient torch waiting at the mouth. "I had hoped you might come, and so I prepared," she whispered, no joy in her smile.

She ducked to enter; I moved to follow, mesmerized at the stone structure leading us beneath the earth.

The stale air smelled of stagnation and death. As Carmilla pulled me forward, the walls grew wider. Skeletons rested on indents in the wall, the plaques of their memories long worn away. Farther, we stepped. More crypts appeared, as well as coffins of stone, many cracked from age.

She stopped within a large clearing, and in a line of coffins, one lay utterly shattered. "This is mine," she said, her voice void of emotion. "Upon my rebirth, I sought to slay my husband, and in recompense he devoted his life to destroying me in death . . . as he had, too, in life. He succeeded by ruining my coffin instead, cursing me to never fully regain strength. Even now, I am crippled. You've seen it. When he died, his children took up his mantle, vowing to bring about my demise, and so on."

Warding away cobwebs, she placed the torch within an ancient, rusted sconce. The room held flickering shadows, yet illuminated Carmilla's smooth skin.

"Carmilla, I have to know the truth." My voice cracked; the day had been long. "The general knew you."

Carmilla's hesitation tore at my shredded heart. "Yes."

"You courted and killed his niece."

"No—"

"Yes!" I screamed, exhaustion and fury and fear all twisting my sanity, fighting for control. "You met her at a ball, you befriended and loved her, you *fed on her and killed her!*" I tugged at my collar, nearly tearing the fabric to reveal the bruise at my breast.

She spoke in rapid tones. "Death is the inevitable end to all things, my darling. And you were close—even the wolves sensed your inevitable change. They fear vampires—"

"From the start, you meant to turn me! Every night while we—" I could not think it, nor speak. Whatever our sin, it was sacred. She had desecrated any purity between us. ". . . you *fed* on me," I spat, betrayal pulling angry tears from my eyes.

"Consider it—what better fate could there be than for you to come with me, loving me unto death, even *hating* me unto death, for at least we would be—" She gasped, though it masked a sob, running forward to me, but stopping, crumbling when I glared. ". . . *together.*"

"Did you claim as much for Bertha, as well? For all your victims?"

"There is much you do not understand—"

"Then tell me!" I cried, furious and broken and torn between the desperate desire to comfort Carmilla and the innate revulsion of her plot, my death only days away—or sooner. "You claimed to love me, but you—"

"I do love you!" she pled, and she collapsed at my feet and wept. Blood stained her hands, her features twisting to match her beastly form. Behind her monstrous visage, I saw a frantic, pitiful girl. "I so desperately love you, my darling, darling." She gazed up at me, full of heartbreak and despair; my own soft heart threatened to yield.

For I still loved her, even now.

"And I have never lied to you," she continued, hands trembling as she clutched at my skirt. I let her, uncaring of the blood staining the cloth. "I have never loved another. I waited for you, for nearly two hundred years."

All that echoed in the empty tomb were my heaving breaths and her tumultuous, desperate sobs. I whispered, "What does that mean?"

"I should not say—"

"*Carmilla*, I will leave!" I shrieked. "Tell me, or watch me walk away!"

Her sobs shuddered and hitched. I thought my skirt might tear from her grip. "Momma said you were my only hope. I died a broken shell. She found me and told me my reason to move forward. She said to know my fate would doom it, but I had *nothing*. I begged to know."

The words were nonsense, yet I clung to them, starved to know the madness of Carmilla's mind.

"Laura, I did not love Bertha. I did not touch Bertha, nor have I touched anyone since the night I came upon you as a little girl—not the way I touch you now. Momma and I have used this ploy a thousand times; vampires must be invited before entering a premise, so rather than scavenge on the streets, we concocted the plan to breach the homes of nobles and feast upon their household.

"Yes, I killed your servant girls. I killed Annette, but only because I must drink to survive—I did not touch them; I did not love them. I intended to kill you." A gasping sob punctuated the statement. She looked up, as though expecting punishment, a supplicant before her master. But I said nothing, the mystery of her words unravelling slowly in my mind. "But only so you could be like me, and stay with me. Forever."

"You would have turned me into a vampire. Like you."

Carmilla nodded against my skirt. Great splatters of blood stained the subtle, pastel pinks.

I stared at the pitiful creature at my feet, not seeing a monster but a lonely, broken girl, one who spoke of magic I did not understand and who gifted a love I craved.

She had not offered an idle future. She truly meant to create one.

"Carmilla—"

Footsteps approached. Light flickered from beyond. I heard the cries of men, and Carmilla immediately stood, grasping me as an entourage of men burst into the room—General Spielsdorf, my father, even the doctor, and others still, making seven in total, all bearing torches and some, weapons. The general wielded a sword and a gun, which he pointed at Carmilla. "Unhand her!"

Fear swept across Carmilla's face. I twisted to stand between them and she. "She does not hold me," I said, feigning bravery, as I had with the wolves. "I stand by her freely."

"Laura, she is not what you think." My father stepped forward, bearing no weapon save for his pleas. "Whatever lies she has told you—"

"Let her go, and she will leave this land." I glanced at her, daring her to deny my claim. Her dark eyes remained wide and watery. "She will leave and never return. There is no need for violence."

The general stepped forward, dropping his torch as he lifted his sword. "I seek recompense. This monster killed my niece."

"And she will kill you, Laura," said an older man. I did not know him, but I recognized his fine coat. Jewels decorated the hilt of his sword. "She has killed countless innocents, destroyed the town over which my castle lies. My great-great-grandfather fought and failed to slay this monster over a century ago—"

"Baron Vordenburg," I said, recalling his name, "your great-great-grandfather all but created her. If you truly desired justice, you would plead for her forgiveness and let her walk away."

When Spielsdorf stepped forward, I moved back, pushing Carmilla with me. "They will not kill me," I whispered, though surely they heard it. "Run."

Spielsdorf rushed, as did Vordenburg. Carmilla shoved me aside.

I stumbled into my father's arms, his iron grip holding me thrall as I watched the scene. I struggled; I screamed. "Release me!"

"Laura—"

"Papa, *please!*"

Before me, Carmilla twisted into a beast, her claws swiping aside the general's sword, only to be bludgeoned across the face by a man wielding a wooden stake. The blast of Spielsdorf's gun ricocheted across the tomb, shaking the very foundation—but did not meet its mark.

Carmilla snarled; they charged her as one. Vordenburg slashed across her arm, and when she threw him aside, another came. Though larger than them all, the men descended upon her like a swarm.

She could smite one, or even two—but here she faltered.

I screamed. *"Papa, no! Please!"*

Father held me in his arms. "Laura, this is what must—"

"No!"

Within the cacophonous scene, I heard a man scream, blood spraying across the wall as Carmilla dragged his flayed body against the stone. Another cried when she tore out his throat, her fangs dripping with gore.

Though I struggled against my father's cage, I felt a flickering of hope. "Carmilla—!"

The beast suddenly writhed, its cry morphing into that of Carmilla's as her body reformed. She gasped, clawing at her chest—from which protruded a wooden stake, held by Baron Vordenburg.

With every second she fought, her strength visibly depleted. I fought to run to her, screaming all the while.

General Spielsdorf approached, sword in hand, chest bloodied and battered. Those that survived stole Carmilla's arms, gripping them as they forced her down to her knees. Vordenburg released the stake; it held. Instead, he grabbed her hair, twisting until she shrieked, forcing her to expose her neck.

Blood splattered when Carmilla coughed, guttural and choking. The general stood before her, sword aloft.

Carmilla stared at him, eyes welling with blood. She did not transform; instead she wept as nothing more than a helpless human girl.

Her fearful eyes matched mine, then they met the sword as it glinted in the firelight. A gasping sob, and she shut them tight.

One strike failed—Spielsdorf's sword stopped partway through her neck. Shrieking, I cried, *"Stop!"*

But to no avail. Another swing—only skin remained.

"Carmilla!"

Already, her eyes had glazed. With a single sweep, the general removed her head—Vordenburg held it up as her body crumpled with a wet, meaty sound.

Still, I struggled; I sobbed. My father held me to his chest, my shoulder wet from his tears, even as they dragged the body from the mausoleum, the head and all. "My Laura, I am sorry," he said, voice quivering. "I know you loved her."

"I loved her," I repeated, anguish in my cries.

"But she did not love you."

"She loved me," I screamed, falling into hysterics. My breathing grew rapid, vision spinning. When my body fell limp, my father gently set me down. I cried upon the dusty floor, struggling for air.

Here lay my heartbreak, nothing to prove of it but bloodstains upon the floor where she had been forced to kneel.

I hardly recall being dragged to my feet. Within the mausoleum, I saw only fog, despair manifesting to cloud my vision.

But my father's arms supported me, pulled me through the dank, dusty path, each step scuffling earth untouched for a hundred years. My very presence desecrated this place, the sacrilege of my entrance bringing violence and death.

Darkness spread before us. I clung to my father's coat, his arm secure around my waist. The other held a torch. Luminous shadows flickered across the trees and castle ruins, and from within the dilapidated display, I saw light beckon, responding to the call of my father's torch.

"General Spielsdorf says they're going to dig a pit within the ruins and burn the body," my father said, amidst the flow of my softly falling tears.

With a gasping sob, I shook my head. "Cremation is abominable before God," I whispered, a perfect recitation of my readings.

"Were she a person in need of burial rites, it would be, but Baron Vordenburg says it is the only way to end a creature of Hell." In his embrace, I crumbled and begin sobbing anew. "Let me take you home, my Laura," he whispered. "I have instructed Madam Perrodon to call the priest—a blessing will remove the sickness from your soul."

"Let me see it done," I said, my words unsteady. "Carmilla was dear to me—"

"She was not Carmilla. She was Countess Mircalla Karnstein—the very same from the portrait in your nightstand. I know she was dear to you—"

"Papa, *please!*" I cried, tugging from his grasp in a final burst of strength. I faced him, my breathing coming in great heaves, but he made no move to grab me—merely watched with pity, his own jaw trembling, struggling to maintain composure.

Amidst our impromptu duel of wills, footsteps from the castle drew our attentions. General Spielsdorf approached. "The pyre is nearly finished," he said to my father, and then he looked to me. "Mademoiselle Laura, you should not be here. You should be home, resting after your scare."

After the violence and slaughter, my heartbreak and tears, there should have been no place for something as petty as 'offense' to raise my hackles, but beneath my flowing tears, my jaw stiffened. I stared, unable to summon any rebuttal, save incredulousness. "My 'scare?'"

"No lady should be subjected to witness a murder," he said, nothing but regret and exhaustion in his eyes. "You should not have seen anything so brutal, and you have my apology."

The sentiment was kind. Perhaps I might have forgiven him someday, but then he continued.

"I do not doubt Mill—*Carmilla* presented the very picture of friendship. She did as much for Bertha, filling her pretty head with sweet affirmations and flattery and . . ." I watched him hesitate, disgust marring his speech. ". . . flirtation, even, and with as beautiful a face as the monster had, anyone would trust her. Even Bertha. Even you."

Each word seemed steeped in poison. My hand gripped my arm, my nails piercing even through the cloth of my dress.

"The baron and I have discussed at length what ploys a vampire will use to lure a victim, the ardor of their affection. Their temptation is often more than any victim can bear to withstand, offering a false and depraved love. But vampires cannot truly love."

Carmilla had loved.

"It is the tragic dichotomy of their nature, that they must destroy what they hold close, often presenting an almost romantic friendship to their victims as they drain them of life. But whatever perverse friendship Carmilla offered you, her passions were unnatural. *Ungodly.*"

Even now, I heard her whisper my name, a prayer for me alone. Carmilla had not believed in God.

"For you to have been coerced by that woman—by that *monster*—does not mean you are beyond repentance."

Spielsdorf withheld blatant accusation of Carmilla and mine's affair, perhaps for my father's sake. But in his face, I saw that he knew. I saw pity and judgement, but with it the promise of understanding, of *redemption* through his willingness to look past my soiled maidenhood.

He would offer his hand all that same. He did not know that I knew, yet still he dared to discount Carmilla's declarations of affection, selfish and misguided as they were.

My words quivered, but not from sorrow, no; my tears had staunched. Instead, I fought to bridle my rage. "General Spielsdorf," I whispered, but still it cut through the stillness of the night, "I thank you for your understanding, and for your concern upon my sullied honor. But the love Carmilla presented to me was—" My father's touch on my back stole my words. I stiffened, knowing I had all but admitted a damning truth.

But there was little now to lose.

"Carmilla's love was more than a perverse temptation." My trembling lip betrayed me now; my breath hitched as I fought to speak. "Carmilla did love me, but not in the way you or the rest of the men could understand, nor in a way you and I could ever share."

We matched eyes, he and I. Spielsdorf gave a curt nod.

Sincerity bled into every plea from my father's lips. "Laura, you cannot be suggesting—"

I stalked away from his touch, past the general who made no move to stop me. Instead, I approached the ruins of Castle Karnstein, toward the radiant light.

Carmilla would die. But I would see her until the end, the only kindness left to give.

Between the shattered walls I stepped, the ceiling fully gone in places, scattered instead about the floor. My feet touched the remnants of polished stone floors, the pattern nearly visible in the flickering light. All about, I saw evidence of grandeur, the home in which Carmilla—*Mircalla*—had lived a sheltered, quiet childhood. The spiraling towers stood cracked, visible from holes in the ceiling. This place would not stand for long—ruined, like its countess.

Centered, I saw the doctor and another man piling wood inside a pit, one clear of any bramble. I saw the genius of their intentions—whatever the state of the castle, there was nothing here to catch fire and burn the forest.

At my approach, Baron Vordenburg, Carmilla's head still clutched in his grasp, held up his free hand. "Mademoiselle—"

"I need to see it for myself," I said, angry tears brimming in my eyes.

His harsh features fell. With a glance behind me, he gave a nod. Turning, I realized my father and the general had followed.

With little ceremony, the baron dropped the head into the man-made hole, as the doctor and another man grabbed the body and dragged it over. "Fear not, Mademoiselle; your nightmare will soon be over. To stake her is the remove her power; to decapitate her is to immobilize her." When a man I did not know offered a torch, Baron Vordenburg accepted and held it above the pit. "To burn her is to kill her; and to scatter her ashes within flowing water promises she will never return."

So my love yet slept?

The baron dropped the torch.

Gasping, I nearly ran to stop it, but my father placed a hand on my shoulder, startling me. I turned to him, his expression utterly void as he watched the pit catch fire.

Then, a knock echoed through the castle ruins.

I turned; we all did, in time to see the shattered door swing open. Standing in the doorway, a woman's silhouette cast a shadow through the fog. Tall but not thin, obscured by fog, she took a single step forward and locked eyes with me.

Time froze. Suddenly, I stood within a pool of light, utter darkness surrounding me beyond.

Another appeared, and within it stood a person I knew, though I had not seen in months—Carmilla's momma.

Breathtaking, her flawless features, age doing nothing to obscure her looks, though she would be my own mother's age if she lived. Opulence dripped from the jewels at her fingers, the necklaces and finery draped across her sensuous form. Her dress bespoke ardor and intention, but her face remained severe. "Would you save her, Laura?"

I stared, shock stifling my tongue.

"If you seek asylum from her advances, let her die in peace."

My hands trembled as I grabbed my skirts. But when I took a step, the light moved with me, and Carmilla's momma came no closer.

"But to save her requires sacrifice. Love is sacrifice, Laura. No sacrifice without blood."

Frantically, I looked about, finally managing to find my words. "What are you?" My words echoed across a void, as though we stood in space. But there were no stars to fill the sky; merely Carmilla's momma to stand as the single planetoid.

"I am a vampire," she said, spreading her arms wide, her lips a deep maroon. "But in life, I was something more—a witch, as you may call it now, respected in my village for my talents in divination. Until the Christians came and carted me away, tortured me until I revealed my allegiance to the devil." Her hands returned to her side, lips pursed. "One will say anything when rats are eating away at their entrails. I was meant for the stake, to burn for my crimes. But by happenstance, while in my prison, I shared a cell with a man whose name I never did find out, who promised me, in exchange for blood, eternal life. I gave it, and when they burned me alive, I awoke within a mass grave and clawed my way to freedom. That was five hundred years ago."

I listened with absolute attention, every word from her lips remarkable—wicked, but remarkable.

"I am not Mircalla's mother," she continued, though that was hardly a revelation. "Instead, I found her over a century ago, utterly fallen into despair, driven only by the animalistic urge to survive, though what remained of her sanity screamed to die. The village she terrorized had been utterly destroyed by her plague, but so had her tomb, shattered by her husband who could not find her. She was nothing more than a crippled beast bleating into the night for death.

"I found her sobbing within the ruins of her coffin, praying for sleep or death—whichever came first. I pitied her, this sad and beautiful little girl, and offered her the chance to come with me, to let me help her find a life among death."

I remembered Carmilla sobbing on the floor, her face full of blood, her broken, shattered stance.

"She refused. She begged me to leave her alone to die or to kill her myself, claimed she had no hope for joy. And so I offered to search her future, to find a hope worth moving on for, but with the warning that to know her fate would take it away. Listless within the crumbled stone, she agreed."

Carmilla had said as much, I recalled, but this woman offered the rest of her cryptic, tearful confession.

"In life, I saw signs within stars, futures within the cards, but in death, I gained a semblance of true power. I touched Mircalla's hand, intention on my mind, to know her greatest hope for joy." Now, the woman looked at me with intrigue, studying me from my feet to my golden hair. "And suddenly I knew you, as though we had been friends for years—your name, your life, your parents, your home. All of it stood in stark clarity in my mind, these memories that were not mine. And so I described you, Laura, to the weeping girl within her grave, told her stories of a little girl not yet born. By the end, Mircalla's eyes held light again."

By now, I sobbed, to think of the brutally slaughtered girl so full of hope. I had seen it myself—when as a little girl, I beckoned her to join me in my bed, later as she clung to me after the disastrous carriage ride, when she kissed me and first called me *darling*.

"I made her swear to say nothing, lest I find out, and lest she destroy the future she already risked with you, merely for knowing. She would woo you as herself, and not as a woman who knew your fate together. I thought she might have a chance—the girl is a romantic fool, but charming in her silly way. Perhaps you might have loved her, even for a moment, let her have a taste of joy before doom came upon her."

My breath caught, my tears streaming down my swollen face.

"Unless you are willing to die in her stead."

The life within me ran cold. My hands clutched each other. "What do you mean?"

"Love requires sacrifice. Would you burn upon the pyre for her?"

My head grew light. I thought I might vomit, so sick my stomach became at the thought. But Carmilla, sweet Carmilla . . . "She would live?"

"That is as much of the future as I may say, lest it no longer come to pass. Mircalla damned her own happiness for a hope to find it. But if you wish to save her, that is all I may say.

"However," she continued, finality in the words, "your choice is your own. Live your life, Laura, knowing you have given her joy unparalleled. She died in sorrow, but she died in peace. You have my gratitude, for she was the daughter I never had. You gave her life again."

The light vanished. I stood within the ruins of Castle Karnstein, looking at the open door. The silhouette had vanished, but all the men ran to investigate our spectral visitor.

I turned around, staring into the inferno. Already, it raged, fueled by wood and perhaps ale, something easily kindled. In trepid measures, I approached, ignoring the confusion behind me, the men oblivious to my thoughts and the vision I'd had.

Heat prickled against my skin, growing fiercer with every step forward. By the edge, I could stare into the fiery pit, the gates of Hell open to my vision. Within, Carmilla's body held its form but quickly seared away, a ghastly vision, her skin steadily eaten by flame. Was this her ultimate fate, to be consumed by Hell's flame? Was there a Heaven for ungodly creatures?

Carmilla had not believed in God. I still did.

I fell to my knees, my hands clasped in silent prayer, my mind muttering not the practiced mantras of youth, but honest words, the first in months. I begged . . . for courage.

"Laura?"

I turned and saw my father.

Something shifted in my resolve as I stared into his visage. My future would have been a pleasant one—shared with a man I hoped was not cruel, bearing his children, and hopefully living a long life in my father's house. And I asked myself, looking not to the Lord nor to man but only to myself, if that were truly what I wanted.

I saw it erupt into flame, burning away at the seams.

I leapt into the inferno.

I once read the words of Dante, who wrote, *"The path to paradise begins in hell."*

Paradise would be my end, it seemed, for this was Hell's great flame.

I felt nothing, save the splintered wood digging into my skin. But I took a breath and became a supernova, combusting from within.

Pain erupted from every pore; my skin tore as it pulled apart. I could not scream for lack of air, nor see for the blinding light and smoke. In my panic and shock, I searched for an escape—instead my hand brushed the charred corpse of my love.

I clung to her, my salvation and my ruin. I felt not the pain of Hell, but two great needles within my breast.

With each failed breath, my world spun faster, even as color disappeared from my vision.

All sight ceased.

All light.

Dark.

(Whatever it takes to save you, my darling, darling . . .)

I awoke to darkness all-consuming.

My fingers skimmed the stone encompassing my body, for I moved freely within my confines. Rough residue of rocks and dust prickled at the back of my head, each shift of my form digging them into my skin. An odd sort of Hell, to die and wake up to, but confined in darkness, trapped within stone, surely I would lose my mind within days.

My God—my body ached from starvation, nausea filling my stomach. Another layer to my torturous confines.

I recalled my fate; I saw my hellish death, Carmilla's burning, headless corpse held between my arms, my skin melting upon contact. Her momma claimed this would be her deliverance, and so I had willingly given my life. To mourn my loss seemed petty, but still I began crying, though I shed no tears. I felt I had no tears left; instead, soul-wrenching sobs echoed about the stone prison.

I would never know Carmilla's fate. She would live. Her mother swore. But I prayed she did not give into despair, even as I did now.

Light blinded me. I gasped, reeling up to cover my eyes, until a feather's touch upon my arm caused my breath to stutter. I heard an angel whisper, *"Awaken, my darling."*

I dared to blink and saw a face as beautiful as sunrise casting a radiant light.

Rather, she carried a torch, but never had I seen a lovelier vision. I surged up, holding her soft form tight between my arms. "Carmilla!" I sobbed, clinging to her perfect form.

Her cries mingled with mine, wetness staining my hair. I could smell it, the blood seeping into my hair, the aroma potent and unmistakable.

Intoxicating, even.

When I finally dared to face her, she had transformed, but to me it no longer held any semblance of monstrosity. It had become merely another facet of her being, another piece of her to admire.

She wore no clothing; I realized that I, too, lay utterly naked. "Carmilla, what has happened?"

Carmilla clung to me with her one free arm. With her lips against my hair, she whispered, "You saved my life. What little remained of me drained what little remained of you."

Carmilla's momma had spoken true.

"The act finished your transformation. I laid you to rest in a coffin and prayed you would rise."

Looking around, I realized I sat within the mausoleum. She held a torch, yet I doubted I needed it—every color stood bright, each sound too loud. My body and soul felt raw and flayed, starved and aware, and so I clung to her, my salvation and damnation. "What of the others? The men."

"Truthfully, I do not know. I rose from my fiery grave and ran. After I circled back to the crypt, I destroyed the entrance. Technically, we're trapped, but with both our strengths, we can escape, my darling."

I pulled away and dared to stand, shaking on my feet, but when Carmilla moved to help, I waved her away. "Let me do this on my own."

And so I stood tall, looking down at my hands, my nails as sharp as my senses. "And so I am . . ?"

"You are a vampire. Like me."

The words did not settle; not yet. Instead, I stole her hand, and together we walked through the maze of tunnels.

It was as Carmilla had promised—though her strength remained sapped, I lifted each boulder with ease, thrust the stones from the entrance, and cleared a path within moments. My nostrils immediately filled with crisp night air.

And blood.

Standing amidst a pile of corpses, I saw Carmilla's momma smile. "Good evening." She held out two bundles of cloth.

Recalling my nakedness, I immediately covered what I could with my hands, but Carmilla stepped forward with no demur and accepted the offering.

When Carmilla handed a dress to me, I wasted no time in stepping into the gathered silk. It was *mine*, I realized, and though I wore no underclothes, I still managed to fill it well enough, once Carmilla tugged a few strings in the back.

Lying before Carmilla's momma, a man groaned. He bore General's Spielsdorf's face, though his stomach had been gored by claws. They were all the men of Carmilla's downfall—the doctor, the baron, the ones I did not know . . .

My father was not among them.

Carmilla's momma reached down and grabbed the wounded general by the hair, blood seeping from his stomach. The man had lost all awareness, it seemed. Seated at death's door, he could not even groan.

The woman held him forward, toward me, and raised a single, expectant eyebrow.

Every instinct yearned to grab him, *consume him*, but revulsion caused me to stumble back. "I cannot," I said, gasping at the words.

A gentle hand caught me. Carmilla cupped my face, some unnamable regret in her dark eyes. "This is the price of life, my darling. No sacrifice without blood. The man will not live, regardless of whether or not you act. But without blood, you will wither away."

I looked away from her and to the fallen man. Carmilla stepped aside as I approached the gruesome offering. At my touch, I felt his pulse, faint as it was, instinct telling me his blood would be rancid once his heart stopped beating. Pressure built in my mouth—my teeth elongated, my own set of fangs.

My bite pierced his flesh, the sinew separating with ease. The warmth that filled me brought no pleasure, but unfathomable relief, the first drink of water after days of dehydration. I would not romanticize it. It disgusted me down to my core. But it was the price I would pay. Once I felt his final breath, I let the general fall, cringing at the blood staining my dress. "Must I kill?" I asked, realizing tears did fill my eyes now.

I wiped my tears, expecting the blotting of red.

"Only selectively," Carmilla's momma said as she offered a hand.

As I stood, Carmilla's hand settled at my waist. "And what of my father?"

"He did not slay Carmilla, and so I instructed him to run."

My father yet lived. Guilt overwhelmed me, to think of his loneliness, his grief. "My father must know." My tears fell faster. Carmilla's momma offered a handkerchief, which I gratefully accepted. "But not yet. Not yet. Someday, I shall write him. On his deathbed, I shall greet him."

"You should write it all, my darling," Carmilla said, her melodious voice soothing my sorrow. "It would look so pretty, forged by your pen."

I shook my head. "And risk our own demise? We cannot be found out."

"Someday there may be a world for us," she whispered, leaning closer to my lips. With my new vision, I saw each delicate eyelash as she fluttered and veiled her eyes. "For now, we shall create our own future."

She pressed her lips to mine, the bitterness of blood staining my mouth, but oh, her kiss tasted of sweetness and hope. "I love you, my Laura."

I loved her so. When I whispered it, she laughed and kissed me again.

A strange new world awaited.

Epilogue

Professor Hesselius closes the journal account, mulling over what she has read. When she checks her phone—*2:45am*—she begins packing her things. Her flight boards in fifteen minutes.

The family of six has gone. The elderly man still snoozes beside her, joined now by a younger man, about twenty-five—a grandson perhaps.

Across from her, the young woman in her wheelchair has set aside *Twilight* in favor of scrolling through her smartphone.

With care to preserve the delicate pages, the professor places the journal back into its plastic wrapping. Surely a work of fiction, a supernatural account written by a closeted young woman in an unenlightened time, crafting a beautiful escapism narrative in the gothic forest scene of Styria. But the story itself is compelling, wrenching in the way history has always been cruel to the minority.

Fantasy or not, the tale would be preserved. As the writer—as Laura, the professor corrects herself—would have wished, the story will be remembered, shared in another time. The world had not been made for them, the vampire girl had said, and the professor smiles to think it could accept their strange and tragic love affair now.

As the professor finishes packing, she notices a smartly-dressed young woman approach, suitcase in tow. From her cropped, gelled blonde hair to her silk, button-down top, she screams of success and subversive culture. The professor has seen her type before—intelligent and vocal, always sparking debates in her classes. The only puzzle piece out of place is the ring upon her left-hand.

The blonde woman kneels before the wheelchair-bound young lady, surprising her with a shameless kiss upon her lips. The professor looks down, unwilling to intrude on their private reunion, when she hears a laugh, and then in perfect French: *"My darling, I worried you would not return before sunrise!"*

The woman merely laughs and kisses her again.

The professor catches a peripheral glance of the lovers as they pass, the blonde woman pushing her companion's chair. She stands, finishing her packing, when she hears:

"Whereas I was more concerned I'd have to stay another night in Germany."

"You only hate it because you could never grasp the language."

Professor Hesselius freezes a moment, but opts to say nothing, shaking her head at her own impossible thoughts. Instead, with care she takes her luggage and the memoir of a lonely French girl, wondering how mad her colleagues would think her if she slept with a cross beside her bed.

Fin.

Further Reading

"Someone will remember us
              I say
              Even in another time"
Sappho, translated by Anne Carson, *If Not, Winter*

"The full-orbed moon with unchanged ray mounts up the eastern sky . . ."
Henry David Thoreau, *The Moon*

"To love or have loved, that is enough. Ask nothing further. There is no other pearl to be found in the dark folds of life."
Victor Hugo, *Les Misérables*

"These violent delights have violent ends. And in their triumph die, like fire and powder, which, as they kiss, consume."
William Shakespeare, *Romeo and Juliet*

"I need thee, oh I need thee."
Annie Sherwood Hawks, *I Need Thee Every Hour*

"The path to paradise begins in hell."
Dante Alighieri, *The Divine Comedy*